P9-DXE-771

"*Stardust on My Pillow* is a brilliantly written anthology. These 'Stories to Sleep On' will move you by their compassionate tone and intriguing characters' lives and will make you want to stay up reading all night! Patsy's writing moved me to apply these themes to my own life and look for a godly outcome."

—THELMA WELLS
AUTHOR AND WOMEN OF FAITH SPEAKER

"No one tells stories as well as Patsy! Now she has transplanted that talent into the world of fiction, and the results are pure gold. *Stardust on My Pillow*, a book of short stories, is long on wisdom. This is a must read."

—STEPHEN ARTERBURN
DIRECTOR, NEW LIFE CLINICS

"I've always known that Patsy is a gifted writer. Now she has opened a new world to us as a marvelous storyteller. You will be charmed, moved, pulled into the lives of these characters that she paints as clearly as the moon on a starry night. Bravo, Patsy!"

—SHEILA WALSH
RECORDING ARTIST AND AUTHOR

"From the moment Pasty burst upon my life in the fall of 1980, I have been dusted with the sparkle of her life. Patsy is a piece of fiction herself... May this be your first fascinating step into her personal land of enchantment."

—FLORENCE LITTAUER
AUTHOR, *PERSONALITY PLUS*

"I rarely read fiction, but when I do…it better be good. Well let me tell you, friends, this is good. It incorporates Patsy's extraordinary communication skills with her unique ability to weave a charming and fantastic story. Plan to stay up late and be dazzled by stardust."

—LUCI SWINDOLL
AUTHOR AND SPEAKER

"Patsy Clairmont captures the reader's imagination with her charming, soothing stories of love and change and life."

—BARBARA JOHNSON
AUTHOR AND SPEAKER

"When Patsy gets a certain twinkle in her eye, you know she's about to tell the kind of story you want to settle in and listen to with an open heart. *Stardust on My Pillow* is brimming with Patsy's eye-twinkling tales. This book will delight you."

—ROBIN JONES GUNN
BEST-SELLING AUTHOR OF THE GLENBROOK
SERIES AND THE CHRISTY MILLER SERIES

"*Stardust on my Pillow* is a delightful collection of stories you should keep on your nightstand. Like a vase holding a spring bouquet, Patsy's book holds a wonderful variety of stories, each one with emotional color and a lingering fragrance all its own. They will give you something to think about, something to laugh about, something to cry about, and if the stardust lands on your pillow just right, something to dream about."

—KEN GIRE
AUTHOR, *MOMENTS WITH THE SAVIOR*
AND *WINDOWS OF THE SOUL*

"Lovely bites of fresh fiction. Good as a bedtime snack—or in between meals!"

—ELISA MORGAN
PRESIDENT AND CEO
MOPS INTERNATIONAL

"Patsy Clairmont has done it again! She's handing you yet another book you'll want to cuddle up to, but this time she's sharing with you her first book of fiction. You'll find wonderfully moving and memorable characters sprinkled throughout the short stories in *Stardust on My Pillow*. You're also going to find them riding around in your head even after you've put the book down. I love that—always a good test of fine writing. Bravo, Patsy."

—MARILYN MEBERG
AUTHOR, *I'D RATHER BE LAUGHING*

"Patsy's short stories are sure to warm your heart and soul. I love the way the truth of Christ is woven into each story in a new way. The characters will make you laugh and even shed a tear or two. Simply one of the most delightful reading experiences I've had in a long time."

—SHELLEY BREEN
MEMBER, CONTEMPORARY CHRISTIAN GROUP
POINT OF GRACE

"Patsy Clairmont has crafted a collection of charming short stories that will not put you to sleep but will send you off to dreamland with a full heart. As endearing as Patsy herself, these honest, poignant tales bring home messages of grace and truth and, above all, hope. Sleep tight."

—LIZ CURTIS HIGGS
AUTHOR, *BAD GIRLS OF THE BIBLE*
AND *BOOKENDS*

"Patsy Clairmont has a sensitive and compassionate voice as a storyteller. Don't miss 'Cloistered'; I was captivated by this tale of a woman incapacitated by agoraphobia. I also especially enjoyed 'Boxed In' and 'Postcards.' I'll look forward to reading the next volume of stories from Patsy."

—FRANCINE RIVERS
BEST-SELLING AUTHOR

"Patsy's manuscript arrived when I was down with the flu. Her pick-me-up stories were a pleasure to read...and I learned men need stardust on their pillows too. Thanks, Patsy."

—NEIL CLARK WARREN, PH.D.
RELATIONAL PSYCHOLOGIST AND AUTHOR

"Patsy's short stories will penetrate your heart and give you hope. She makes you realize what is important in life as only Patsy Clairmont can so wonderfully do!"

—DR. KEVIN LEMAN
PSYCHOLOGIST

STARDUST
ON MY PILLOW

STARDUST
ON MY PILLOW

Stories to Sleep On

PATSY
CLAIRMONT

WATERBROOK
PRESS

STARDUST ON MY PILLOW
PUBLISHED BY WATERBROOK PRESS
2375 Telstar Drive, Suite 160
Colorado Springs, Colorado 80920
A division of Random House, Inc.

Scripture taken from the *New American Standard Bible*® (NASB).
© Copyright The Lockman Foundation 1960, 1962, 1963,
1968, 1971, 1972, 1973, 1975, 1977. Used by permission.

The characters and events in this book are fictional, and any resemblance
to actual persons or events is coincidental.

ISBN 1-57856-369-0

Copyright © 2000 by Patsy Clairmont

All rights reserved. No part of this book may be reproduced or transmitted
in any form or by any means, electronic or mechanical, including photocopying
and recording, or by any information storage and retrieval system, without
permission in writing from the publisher.

WATERBROOK and its deer design logo are registered trademarks of WaterBrook
Press, a division of Random House, Inc.

Library of Congress Cataloging-in-Publication Data
Clairmont, Patsy.
    Stardust on my pillow : stories to sleep on / Patsy Clairmont. — 1st ed.
        p. cm.
    ISBN 1-57856-369-0
        1. Christian fiction, American. I. Title.

PS3553.L227 S7 2000
813'.54—dc21   00-021926

Printed in the United States of America
2004

10 9 8 7 6 5 4 3

When I was thirteen years old,
the most wonderful miracle occurred in my family's home:
My parents presented me with a beautiful baby sister,
Elizabeth Ann. Once, as a toddler,
she assembled household items to form steps
so she could climb onto the kitchen counter. From there she
maneuvered over to the sink and guzzled half a bottle of shampoo.
Yes, from the beginning I was smitten with this
wonderful, willful child who was full of
imagination and mischief.

———————

TO ELIZABETH,
who continues to delight me with her flair

CONTENTS

CHATTANOOGA

CHOO-CHOO

*E*very afternoon at three o'clock Papaw sat under the weeping willow tree in his front yard and played the "Chattanooga Choo-Choo" on his harmonica. It was a Kentucky tradition—or at least it was a tradition for him. That's how Papaw remembered his dad, Jamie Lee Cole.

Jamie Lee had been a miner who worked hard and died young from black lung. He was only thirty-eight when he left Papaw, then "Little Jamie," a fatherless boy. Little Jamie was ten and in need of a man's firm influence, but Jamie Lee was gone and there was nothing anyone could do about it, least of all Little Jamie.

Sadie, Jamie's momma, grieved something fierce. She stopped eating until her clothes hung like sacks and her lovely hair thinned and lost its sheen. Some days she didn't get out of bed except to take the path out back. Little Jamie would try to coax her to eat, but to no avail. Sometimes he would sit up all night at her bedside to make sure she didn't die too. He had heard it said that orphan boys were sent to work camps where they were beaten and starved. Jamie thought losing his daddy was about as much pain as he could endure.

Concerned about his momma and his own future, Little Jamie set about finding her a cure. He had heard tell of a woman near Nebo who had the Jesus touch in her hands, and he decided to fetch her.

❧

"Howdy. Is anybody home?" Jamie called out from behind some thorny shrubs. He was hoping to get a look at Miss Pearl, the healing woman, before he showed himself.

Neither answer nor movement came from the small cabin in the clearing. The loud silence spooked Jamie, and when a titmouse chirped nearby, Jamie nearly jumped into the bushes. Several thorns caught his shirt and tore at his skin.

"Ouch!" he yelled as he pulled away from his hiding place.

"Well, howdy to you," a voice called out from behind him.

Startled, Jamie jumped backwards and found himself once again entangled in the picker shrubs. This time Jamie was in too much pain to be scared. "Don't you know you shouldn't sneak up on people?" he bellowed as he spun around to face the stranger. "Oh, m-my, I'm s-sorry."

A wee woman not four feet tall with hair the color of copper stood before him. He wondered if she was an elf.

"It's okay," she assured him. "Have you come seeking Miss Pearl? She'll be back soon. Come sit on the porch, and I'll get you some salve for your arm. My name is Penny. My daddy said I wasn't big enough to be worth a plug nickel so they named me Penny. Momma said I was a bad penny at that, which is why I guess they gave me to Miss Pearl when I was five years old. Anyhow, it was the best thing that ever happened to me because Miss Pearl knows how to love folks no matter their size."

Jamie realized this lady might be small in stature, but she was tall on words. He never had met anyone who could talk without taking a breath. And Jamie had never met an adult who was shorter than he was. Yet Penny made Jamie feel as if they were already friends.

At the mention of his arm he looked down and noticed the tear in his shirt sleeve and the warm trickle of blood soaking his skin. "Nah, it's okay," he answered, embarrassed that he had done battle with a bush.

"Never you mind. Follow me. Miss Pearl would be disheartened if I didn't see to our guests. When she's not here, I'm in charge, and it's important to me that I carry out her example. She's a caring woman. Yes, a real servant to others. Why, folks around these parts thinks mighty highly of her. I think that's because she's more full of Jesus than she is of herself."

Jamie followed Penny with her flurry of words and her short, quick strides as she made her way to the porch.

"Have a seat, young man. I'll be right back. It won't take me anytime, and I'll tend to those picker bites. Picker bites is what my granny used to call them. Granny died near three years ago. Sure do miss her. Miss Pearl was real fond of Granny too…" Penny climbed the steps and entered the cabin still talking, then closed the door behind her.

Jamie sat on the porch step and took in his surroundings. A pump housed in a little open-sided shanty stood nearby. A dipper tied on a string dangled from the pump handle. Wood was piled in neat stacks at the end of the porch. A blue-and-white speckled tin pitcher and bowl hung from nails on the railing. Black-eyed Susans crowded around the edge of the cabin, and sweet Williams nested near the woodpile. Pots of ferns and several rocking chairs shared the porch's shade, adding friendliness to the place. The cabin was made from hand-hewn white pine logs, and, while not a fancy place, Jamie found it inviting.

The latch on the door behind Jamie lifted, and he turned to see Penny approaching him. "Hold out your arm, and I'm goin' to fix you up," she instructed him.

Penny's smile disarmed any hesitancy on Jamie's part, and he held out his arm. She poured some water over it to cleanse the wounds, and then Penny squeezed a clear, gooey substance from a piece of a broken plant onto the punctures. "There, that ought to do it. You'll be good as new by tomorrow, I betcha."

"What is that gooey stuff?"

"Miss Pearl just calls it 'the balm.' It's a soother of pain. It takes the sting out and keeps infection from causing the wound to get all inflamed."

"Can it help heart pain? My mom needs help. Ever since my daddy died she says her heart hurts like it's broken. She won't eat, and she's lookin' kind of scrawny."

"No, this won't soothe that kind of pain, but I'm sure Miss Pearl will know how to help. By the way, you haven't told me your name."

"Jamie. Jamie Cole from Pike's Cove."

Just then a whistle pierced the air. Penny jumped up and grabbed a wooden whistle from the cushion on one of the rockers and responded. Then she looked at Jamie with happiness all over her face and announced, "It's Miss Pearl! She'll be here in a few minutes. We use the whistles to let each other know we're on our way. We whittled these whistles ourselves; aren't they beauties? And they all sound different, too; some like birds and others like trains. We made them out of cedar and pine that we cut from over by the Orange Water Crick. Miss Pearl said the water's orange 'cause it's rich in ore, but other folks think it turned that way 'cause of all the feudin' between the Bakers and the Cromwells. They say a Cromwell shot Merry Lynn Baker when she was crossing the crick, and her spilled blood colored the water forever. Cromwells swore the shooting was an accident; they mistook Merry Lynn for a deer. But I believe Miss Pearl; it's those ore nuggets that's turned that water orange as an ol' punkin."

Jamie felt his stomach tighten in anticipation of Miss Pearl's arrival. He wondered if she would be a wee woman too. Most of all he wondered if she would help his mom.

Within moments Jamie saw a form step out of the woods and into the clearing. As she moved closer, Jamie realized she was anything but wee. Miss Pearl was taller than Jamie's daddy had been, and he had stood near six feet in height. Her face was brown from the sun, and her hazel eyes smiled with warmth. Miss Pearl's chestnut hair peeked out from her straw hat in frizzy wads. She was dressed in work britches, boots, and a flannel shirt.

Jamie thought Miss Pearl looked handsome, like a grand tree. And her rich voice seemed to washed over him with acceptance when she said, "How nice. We have company."

"Yes, this is Jamie, Jamie Cole from Pike's Cove. He's here about his mama. She's got a broken heart cause Jamie's daddy died. I been carin' for him 'cause he jumped smack-dab in the middle of that picker nest over yonder and near pulled off his arm on those thorns. But I slopped him up good with the balm; he'll be healin' in no time."

"Hello, Jamie. Thank you for coming by. Do I know your mom?"

"No ma'am. I don't think so. My dad died three months ago, and she's been doing poorly ever since. I heard you had healin' in your hands, and I thought maybe you could help her." Jamie felt his voice quiver and a pressure form in his chest. He stood very still, afraid he might burst.

"Penny, would you put on some tea for us?"

When Penny closed the cabin door, Miss Pearl turned back toward her rigid guest. "Come here, lad. Don't be afraid of your loss. Your grief will rise up inside you unexpectedly; it's simply feelings that need to be expressed. Come allow me to hold you for a moment."

Jamie stared at her open arms as he felt his pain move up into his throat and form into sobs. The next thing he knew, she was rocking him in her generous arms, assuring him of God's love while he wept.

After a few minutes, Jamie pulled away, embarrassed to have shown so much emotion to a stranger. His daddy had told him when he was dying that Jamie would have to be brave. And he had been. This was the first time since the funeral he had cried.

"Don't feel awkward, Jamie. Grief visits us all. Even Jesus wept. And what better way to get to know each other than to share important feelings? Your dad's death was an important event in your life. It will be a way-marker for your path."

"A way-marker?"

"Yes. Isn't there a signpost telling you how to get back to Pike's Cove?"

"Yes, there are two. One near Moss Bluff and one nailed on a tree near Pillow Crick."

"Well, as sure as those signs will lead you home, the signs your daddy left you will guide you into manhood. A way-marker is like a signpost telling you which way to go. And depending on how you take in your daddy's life and death will affect how you live out your life."

Jamie understood signs. He and his daddy left signs in the woods when they hunted. They would bend twigs, pile rocks, or carve a mark on a tree with a pocketknife.

Signs were important in the woods and in the caves, too. Jamie's dad had told him that all the miners paid close attention to the canaries that were kept in the tunnels. If they fell over in their cages, it was a sign the air wasn't safe, and the men should get out fast.

Jamie hadn't thought about his dad's leaving him signs to follow, but somehow the idea made him feel less alone.

Penny returned with their tea and some toasted raisin bread. "I iced the tea and heated the bread. Nothin' like cold and hot to warm one's innards. And there's more if this isn't enough. I made four loaves of bread before daybreak just hopin' company would drop by. And what do you know, in comes Jamie. Isn't the Lord good!"

The bread's lovely aroma reminded Jamie that he hadn't eaten anything except for a handful of wild berries when he hiked past Pillow Crick hours earlier.

Miss Pearl bowed her head. "Lord, You've sent us Jamie today, and we are so pleased that You'd do that for Penny and me. Thank You. Bless this offering of food and prayers. The food's for us, the prayers are for You, Lord. What a sweet exchange. Bless Jamie's mama and us as well. Our cups are overflowin' because of You. Amen."

"Will you come see my mom?" Jamie asked Miss Pearl with pleading eyes when she looked up.

"Yes. Yes, of course we will. Very soon."

After Jamie ate three slices of raisin bread and gulped his cup of chamomile tea, he rose to leave.

Miss Pearl said to him, "Jamie, I want you to take this whistle, and one day soon you'll hear me blow mine, and you can answer back."

For a moment a sparkle kindled in Jamie's sad eyes as he laid hold of the whistle. Then, stuffing it in his pocket, he lit out on the path home. He ran through the woods like a deer, darting down one path after another until he reached Pillow Crick. There he sat a spell dangling his feet in the water and thinking on the women of Nebo—Penny, full of words and friendliness, and Miss Pearl, full of warmth and wisdom. Jamie felt something begin to grow inside of him. He wasn't sure, but he thought it might be hope.

Crackling brush behind him caused Jamie to spin around in time to see Mr. Campbell, a neighbor, with his coon dog, Plug, step onto the path near the water.

"Boy, we been lookin' for you. You better git home. Your mama's plum sick. Doc's with her, but she's puny lookin'. You better run, Jamie."

The news felt like someone had thrown a bucket of crick water on the kindlin' of his hope. Jamie ran faster than he had ever run before, like a jackrabbit outrunning a sly fox. By the time he started up the hill toward home, he was panting hard and his heart was jumping. Folks were milling about on the porch like when his daddy died. Fear gripped him hard, and he stopped in his tracks. Mrs. Campbell waved him onto the porch and told him to go in quietly.

Mom was pale as new milk, and she lay so still. Jamie stood at the foot of the bed wishing someone would tell him if she were alive or dead. He couldn't tell, and he couldn't bring himself to ask.

Finally the doc said, "Jamie, your momma will need you to stay by her side and tend to her. Mrs. Campbell will check on you from time to time, and I'll be back tomorrow. If you need me sooner, you ring the church bell, and I'll come a runnin'." The doctor leaned down and whispered something in Sadie's ear and then left.

Before long everyone meandered off until Jamie was alone with his fragile mom. He wanted to cry out, "Don't leave me. I'm too little to do this alone."

That thought guided him to better days when his daddy was still alive and they had gone hunting. Jamie's dad told him to stand in an opening while his dad flushed out some deer. When the deer ran in Jamie's direction, he was supposed to jump up and down, hootin' and hollerin'. A look of concern flooded through him after the plan was laid out.

"What's a matter Jamie?" his dad asked.

"I'm too little to do this alone," Jamie protested.

"C'mere, son." His dad beckoned Jamie close to him. "The best way to grow out of small is to stand up tall. You don't have to feel brave to act brave. Besides, you holler loud enough, those deer will think you're the Chattanooga Choo-Choo and hightail it away from you."

Jamie laughed hard that day at the thought of his being the Chattanooga Choo-Choo. And things went just as his dad said they would. The deer came, Jamie hollered loud enough to be heard clear over to Plum Hollow, and those deer circled back right into the path of his waiting daddy. That winter when folks mentioned how he had grown, Jamie was certain he was growing out of small.

Now Jamie whispered over his momma's bed, "I think this is a way-marker." In his head he heard his dad's voice say again, "The best way to grow out of small is to stand tall. You don't have to feel brave to act brave." Jamie was heartened and moved over to his mom's side.

"Momma," he said quietly.

Sadie didn't move.

"Momma," Jamie repeated with more determination.

Her eyelashes fluttered, and then she looked up at her son. Pity filled her eyes and spilled over into tears that dampened her pillow.

"It's okay, Mom. I'm here. You're not alone. Can I get you anything?"

Sadie's lips formed a no, and then she fell back asleep. Jamie took out his whistle and wished he could blow it loud enough that Miss Pearl could hear back in Nebo. If only she would come, maybe, just maybe, she could help.

Boy, there's times you'll just need to do what needs to be done. The thought came so clear Jamie turned to see who said it, and then he realized it was his daddy's voice in his head. Jamie remembered when a snake, hidden in the woodbin, had bitten his dad. There wasn't time to find the doctor, so his dad tied off the wound with his hankie, used his pocketknife to cut an opening, sucked out the poison, and spat it on the ground. The memory still caused Jamie to shudder. Yet he saw in his mind that his dad had no choice, and he did what he had to do.

Jamie found comfort in remembering his dad's strengths, and the things Jamie had learned from him then now seemed to hold more immediate value. It was just like Miss Pearl said; his daddy had left him signs to follow.

Jamie sat and pondered a good while, trying to decide what he should do for his mom. Then he remembered what Penny and Miss Pearl had done to make him feel some better, and he put on the teakettle. He couldn't find any chamomile tea in the cupboard, but he located some peppermint, catnip, and spearmint teas; so he took a little of each and put it in the teapot. Next he added some honey because he remembered someone saying it was good for the "flus and the blues." He knew his momma had the worst case of the blues he had ever seen.

Once the water boiled, Jamie poured it into the teapot and let it steep. He pulled out Sadie's favorite teacup from the cabinet and carefully filled it. While the tea cooled some, Jamie dug through his dad's toolbox until he unearthed his harmonica. Jamie tapped it against his leg to get out the dust and gently blew into it. Then he slipped it in his shirt pocket.

Once he carried the teacup to the bedside, he jostled his mom's arm until she opened her eyes. "Mom, it's time to be brave. I've made you some tea to give you strength, and you need to sip on it." Before she could say no, Jamie slid another pillow behind her head and edged the cup to her lips. "C'mon, Mom, just a sip."

Sadie parted her lips and took a swallow and then closed her eyes.

"That was good, Momma. Now I need you to stay awake for just a little while. I want to tell you about Daddy's way-markers, and the wee woman Penny, and Miss Pearl who is as tall as our blue spruce out back."

Jamie rattled on and on, interspersing his animated story with sips of tea for his mom. Most of the time Sadie kept her eyes closed, but every once in a while she would lift her lids just long enough to glimpse her son. Then Jamie took out the harmonica and played a few simple songs his dad had taught him.

Exhausted from his day, Jamie leaned against the side of his mom's bed and dozed off. Twice in the night his mom's hand touched his head, causing him to jump. Both times she motioned for a little water, and he held her head while she sipped.

Saddened by her pale skin, just before daybreak, Jamie knelt down and prayed, "Lord, my dad told me once that You speak to a person's heart. Would You please tell my mom's heart how much I need her? She can't seem to hear me. Thank You kindly. Amen."

Jamie was fixing his mom some tea at about eight in the morning when he heard the rooster crow. Then another sound cut through the air. Jamie froze. Then he heard it again. It was Miss Pearl's whistle.

He grabbed his whistle, ran out onto the porch, and blew a hardy reply. Then, to make sure, he blew the whistle again.

Within minutes he spotted the wee one and her giant friend making their way up the hill. Jamie was beside himself. He didn't know if he should dance or cry. Instead he flew to meet them, telling them of his mom's weakened condition even before they could hear him. When Jamie neared Miss Pearl, she placed her hand on his shoulder, and he began to settle down.

Inside the house Miss Pearl bent over Sadie and gently placed her hand on the woman's head. Sadie looked up.

"Hello, Sadie. I'm Miss Pearl. Jamie tells me you've been heartsick. I hope you'll allow me to be your friend. It looks like your son could use a friend too. He's a mighty fine boy. You must be real proud. I've brought you some fixin's for your tea that I believe will help you some."

Sadie looked at the tall woman, the wee one, and then at Jamie with questioning eyes.

"It's just like I told you, Momma. Please let Miss Pearl help you," he pleaded.

"Jamie, would you heat some water, and, Penny, would you help tidy up the kitchen? Sadie and me are going to visit a spell."

"C'mon, Jamie, you and me will get that kitchen lookin' spiffy in no time. By the way, I whittled you a spankin' new whistle. I even twisted you up a string so you can wear it around your neck. That way you won't lose it. The whistle sounds like a hoot owl after sunset, if I do say so myself. You can try it out after we've tended to our chores." Penny rattled on as the two of them moved into the kitchen.

For the next three days, Miss Pearl stayed at Sadie's bedside, reading, reciting Scripture, and administering her teas. Jamie's favorite activity was when they would all sing to his mom, everything from "Camptown Races" to "Amazing Grace." In the late evening hours, Jamie could hear Penny and Miss Pearl praying over his mom even as she slept.

By the fourth morning, Sadie was sitting up a few hours a day sipping broth and talking, finally talking. Color had begun to ease back into her face, and from time to time she would smile.

On day six Sadie walked to the porch, sat in a rocker, and spoke of her and Jamie's future. That was when Miss Pearl announced that she and Penny would have to head back to Nebo.

Jamie knew the day would come sooner than he wanted, but he had prepared parting gifts for his friends. Every day after dinner Jamie had gone up to the Campbells' to work on his surprises.

His daddy had told him once, when the neighbors had helped him pull his mule out of the swamp, "Son, never let a kindness go unattended." That winter his dad made each neighbor a new bridle.

When Miss Pearl and Penny were saying their good-byes, Jamie vanished around the corner of the house. Within minutes he reappeared, dragging a burlap bag for Penny.

She clapped her small hands together with glee at the thought of a gift. When she pulled open the drawstring, she found a small wooden stepstool with the letters *G-O-L-D* carved on it. Mr. Campbell had helped Jamie make the stool in trade for some chores Jamie would tend to when his mom was up and about.

"It's wonderful, Jamie, but why does it say *gold?*" Penny asked.

"'Cause your daddy was wrong about you not bein' worth a plug nickel. You are pure gold to me."

Penny was so moved by his expression of love that for the first time in a long time she was without words.

Jamie ran back to the side of the house and pulled out another sack for Miss Pearl.

"Now, Jamie, you didn't make me a stepstool did you?" Miss Pearl asked.

They all laughed at the thought that she would need any additional height.

What she found in her sack was a sign made from peeled birch cut in the shape of an arrow. It read, "This is the way, walk ye in it."

"Oh, Jamie, I love it."

"It's a way-marker, Miss Pearl. My mom helped me pick a verse, and Mrs. Campbell helped me with the printing, but I cut the birch off that tree over yonder and peeled it myself."

"Jamie, I will keep it always. I will post it on my porch so every day I will be reminded of my friend Jamie and also my friend Jesus, who guides me from one way-marker to another. Come here, lad, let me hold you before I go."

Jamie paid many visits to Nebo over the next ten years until his way-markers led him to a town faraway. Word came that Miss Pearl had gone home to glory. She requested that Jamie's way-marker be hung over her grave site. Several years later Penny stepped into the arms of a heavenly Father who valued her greatly.

Sadie outlived them both and spent her years helping those who grieved, until one day on her way to the church she sat down under a willow and fell asleep. The folks who found her said she was smiling. Jamie wasn't surprised. She had waited a long time for that day.

Jamie married a city girl, who walked in the ways of the Shepherd, and they had a sheepfold of children. Jamie was a schoolteacher who taught his students and his own children the importance of way-markers every chance he had. The years collected up for Jamie into decades, and his younguns presented him with younguns who called him Papaw.

And Papaw could be heard every afternoon at three under the willow playing his harmonica. When he would get done, he would tap it against his knee to get all the dust out and slip it into his shirt pocket. Then he would sit and think on his boyhood when his daddy had him a hootin' and a hollerin' in the woods as if he were the Chattanooga Choo-Choo. And Papaw would laugh and laugh.

POSTCARDS

Dear Ella,

Please send my blue parka. The bears made mincemeat out of the black one, but good fortune allowed me to disrobe before they grabbed it. A morning run can be so invigorating, and I'm grateful to say, the tree I shimmied up was too narrow for the bears to join me...that or the Hershey's bars in the parka pocket satisfied their sweet tooth.

Hope you and Char had a good time at the circus.

Don't forget to check on Sly. He mopes when he is ignored.

JW

Dear JW,

Why didn't you mention Sly was a python? I thought you said he was a pig. Char fainted and I screamed when we went to check on him and discovered his slithering identity. Finally your elderly neighbor, Mrs. Wagner, came and rescued us both. Mrs. Wagner has agreed to feed him while you're away since neither Char nor I am up to the job.

The circus was fine until Char became tickled at the clowns' antics and in a knee-slapping moment snorted a popcorn kernel up her nose. We spent the next three hours at the hospital waiting to have it extracted.

I couldn't find your parka...Perhaps Sly ate it.

Ella

P.S. Is Mrs. Wagner's hair always that orange?

Ella,

I said Sly can eat a pig, not he is a pig. And Sly doesn't like parkas—not enough roughage.

Mrs. Wagner scares Sly with her iridescent hair, but I guess it will be okay for her to feed him for a while.

How's Char's nose? That ought to cure her of snorting.

Would you check in the storage bin behind the garage for my parka? It's chilly here in upstate New York at night, and covering up with branches has its disadvantages.

By the way, when you attend Mom's birthday party, give her my best.

JW

JW,

Tell me you didn't know a condominium of mice live in your storage building. I hate mice! You know that, baby brother, and I don't appreciate your torturing me; we aren't children anymore.

Really, JW, you need to grow up. Instead of playing in the woods like some Tarzan wannabe, you should come home and take care of your own dumb snake. Besides, you should be here for Mom's birthday. You owe her that.

Speaking of owing, I bought you a new parka at the discount store and shipped it this afternoon. You owe me $14.95.

Ella

Dear Urp,

What do you mean you don't like mice? I can still
see you sporting those Mickey Mouse ears around the
neighborhood when we were growing up. Lighten up.

Tarzan? What planet are you from, sister? I'm
Rambo material.

Mom understands my missing her party. You're just jealous
'cause she likes me best.

I owe you?! Ha! Take it off the bumper and windshield I had to
replace after you rear-ended that sanitation truck with my car. Not to
mention the fumigation bill tagged on after half the garbage of our fair
city ended up pouring through the windshield into my front seat. I'm
still picking rice out of my vents.

JW

P. S. By the way, would you add my name on your gift for Mom? I'll
pay you later.

JW,

Rambo? You mean Dumbo, don't you? You're twenty-five years old. Pack up your loincloth, Tarzan, and come home.

When are you going to stop harping about that car accident? Imagine what a painful memory it is for me. I was the one covered in coffee grounds, shredded lasagna, and moldy cheesecake. I haven't been able to eat cheesecake since, and you know it was my favorite. Besides, don't you think "car" is a rather generous term for that old rust bucket of yours? Anyways, the insurance company picked up the expense for most of the repairs.

Mom loved us all the same. I asked her. Enough said.

If you call me "Urp" again, I shall address all your mail to Jehosophat Willerd Wicket III. Your name alone should be a statement about Mom's affections.

Ella

P.S. Char and I baked you cookies; they should arrive soon.

Ella,

You actually asked Mom if she loved me best? Give me a break. I said that as a joke. You know, like "ha-ha." C'mon, where's your sense of humor?

By the way, my car wouldn't be a rust bucket if the salt from the garbage spill hadn't eaten off the paint. And the insurance only paid half the damages; who do you think picked up the rest?

You know my name was Great-Grandmother's fault, not Mom's choice, but how do you explain Urpella Thanie Wicket? Not exactly what I would call a term of endearment.

Char helped with the cookies? I chipped a tooth on her last ones. Our little sister isn't exactly Martha Stewart, in case you hadn't noticed.

Thanks, my parka arrived today. What's with the bowling pins emblazoned across the back?

JW

Jehosophat Willerd,

What do you mean, I can't cook? I prepare
food at the school cafeteria three days a week, for
your information. It wasn't my fault I lost one of
the stones from my ring in that cookie batter.

Come to think of it, those stones were from the ring you gave
me when I graduated from high school. You should be grateful I
still wear it. Or did wear it. When I noticed a stone was missing,
I took it to the jeweler's, and he told me the pinpoint rubies
weren't rubies at all. Imagine my embarrassment. If you had
bought the real thing, it wouldn't have fallen apart, and you
wouldn't have a chipped tooth. So, as usual, big brother, you bit
off more than you can chew.

And I didn't appreciate the snide remark about my snorting.
A person can't help her laugh. Your braying isn't all that
attractive either.

By the way, I know how you came up with the rest of the
money for your car repairs—me. Exactly when are you going to
pay me back? Maybe I could sell Sly to a zoo for your first
payment.

Char

Charjean Viola,

Hello, little sister. How nice to hear from you. I hope you're well too. You did ask, didn't you, or was I reading between the lines on that one?

I think you do many things well. Cooking just doesn't happen to be one of them. What's the big deal? I know you didn't mean to chip my tooth, but guess what? You did. Just deduct my dental work off my car debt, and we should be close to even.

Now, about your ring. What happened to "it's the thought that counts"? Besides, you wouldn't believe how many boxes of Cracker Jacks I had to eat before I found that ruby ring. Char, you knew I wasn't working then. What did you expect, Tiffany's?

I'm rather fond of your laugh, but you have to admit inhaling popcorn for a pastime is a little bizarre.

I wouldn't try to sell Sly, if I were you. He has a fondness for red-headed, snippet sisters who snort. He-haw, he-haw.

JW

JW,

Char got your card. She's not laughing. After all, she has enough going on without your pushing her buttons. John has asked for a divorce, and Char thinks he has a girlfriend. Not only is her heart broken, but she also can't figure out how she and the children will survive financially on what she makes at the cafeteria. John put their home on the market, and Char is in such turmoil she isn't sure which way to turn.

By the way, we canceled Mom's party. The excitement was too much for her, and her blood pressure started to climb. I'm taking her to see Dr. Swartz this afternoon as a precaution.

I tossed a coin to choose between bowling pins or crossbones on your parka. I went with the pins...be grateful.

Did you get the cookies, Ramboni?

Ella

Dear Char,

I contacted Mrs. Wagner, and she has removed Sly
from my house so you and the kids can stay there. I
won't be home for another month, but when I get
back, we will work something out. There's room for us
all.

I stashed some cash in the flour canister in the pantry. Help
yourself. I have more. Honest.

It may take time, but this will work out.

JW

Ella,

Keep me posted on Mom...and Char.

Yes, the cookies arrived, and they were great. Let
me rephrase that. The ones I ate were great. I'm not
sure how the raccoons felt about them. I arrived back
at my camp after rescuing some folks who flipped their canoe in the
river and found a family of coons polishing off the last morsels. I
yelled to scare them away, and the largest coon scampered for the
woods and then stopped, looked over his shoulder at me, and believe
it or not, smiled. It appeared to be the grin of a satisfied customer.

JW

Dear JW,

I don't know what to say except thanks. John has a buyer for the house who wants immediate occupancy, so it looks like I'll have to take you up on your offer. The last time I felt this way was when we were kids, and you swung around with that two-by-four, accidentally hit me in the stomach, and knocked the breath out of me. I feel numb one moment and engulfed in pain the next. This past week I've cried a river...and guess what? I snort when I cry, too.

The invitation to stay in your home was a balm to the gaping hole in my broken heart.

Love, Char

JW,

Mom's appointment with Dr. Swartz proved eventful. While the good doctor was taking Mom's blood pressure, he unexpectedly stepped back onto my foot and broke my toe. I screeched in pain, which caused him to leap forward and lose his balance. He fell against the door and sprained his wrist. Just then the nurse, having heard me bellow, flung open the door, which catapulted the doctor onto my lap. Something came over Mother, and she began to guffaw until she developed the most annoying case of the hiccups, which hung on for an hour.

The good news: Mom's blood pressure is down.

JW, what you did for Char was generous and thoughtful.

Ella

P.S. Where's Sly?

Ella,

Thanks for the details on your medical escapade.
I, too, laughed myself into the hiccups. I can see it
now: rotund Dr. Swartz in your petite lap with skinny
Mom in a hospital gown, chortling between hiccups.
Are you sure you weren't on *Candid Camera*?

Speaking of cameras, I need mine. Would you send it please? I've
met someone, and I wanted to send a picture of her to you and Char.

My buddy Ralph offered to sell Sly for me, but Mrs. Wagner felt
she and Sly had bonded, and she decided to keep him. Imagine, my
eighty-five-year-old, orange-haired neighbor with her own fifteen-foot
python. I'm about to get another case of the hiccups just thinking of it.

JW

P. S. Hope your toe is better.

Dear Brother,

Your home is working out nicely for us. Thank
you again. The kids are having trouble
understanding why Daddy has left us, but then so
am I...so am I. Dismantling a family is very sad.

Eventually I will receive part of the money from the house
sale, and then I will be able to rent a place of our own. But I'm
not sure how long before that money will come through. I don't
want to take advantage of your hospitality.

What's this I hear about a girlfriend?

Love, Char

Dear Char,

You stay at my home as long as you need to. John
has to be a jerk to leave you and the kids. You were a
good wife to him, and you are a terrific mom. I'm sorry
he has hurt you so.

Remember when we were kids and life was too painful? We'd
make a beeline for Dad, and he'd tend to our problems. Somehow he
knew exactly what to do. Well, my friend Cyndi says God wants to be
that kind of father and more to us.

I've had a lot of time to think and even to pray out here in the
woods. Yes, your brother prays. I don't have things figured out, but I
have a growing sense that our lives were meant to have divine
purpose. What do you think?

Love, JW

P. S. My girlfriend is fine, thank you. (Smile)

JW,

I no longer use a cane to hobble about so I'm improving. Glad I could provide you with some entertainment. Actually, I'm still chuckling myself. That is, when my toe isn't throbbing. Mom still titters over the incident; it seems to have added a glint to her eyes. She said it was a lot better than a stuffy birthday party.

Who is this girl you spoke of, JW? Aren't you in the wilderness? Has Tarzan found Jane? Fill us in. Your sisters are eager to know.

I mailed your camera, but you'll notice I took a couple of shots on the roll of film first. They are of Mrs. Wagner and Sly. Forgive the glare; I took the pictures through the window. I thought you might want to see that the "odd couple" is doing fine. Note Mrs. Wagner's new green hairdo. I thought the spikes were a bit much, but, hey, Sly seems content with his spunky owner.

Warmly, Ella

Dear Sisters,

Cyndi is twenty-three and is a nurse. Her parents are missionaries and are home on furlough from India. I met them when their canoe capsized, spilling them and some of their belongings in the drink. When I heard their shouts, it was Ramboni to the rescue. After they dried out at my campfire, they invited me to join them for some fireside chats that have led to a warm friendship with them.

I know, I know, you two want to know what she looks like. Cyndi is five foot three, with sparkling blue eyes and short, curly, black hair. She's a delightful mix of my two favorite sisters. I really care for her. Pictures coming soon.

JW

Dear JW,

My emotional pain is consuming, and all I've wanted is Daddy. I know if he hadn't died, he would have helped me pull my thoughts together. Losing John has helped me understand Mom's losses better. I thought at the time of Dad's death that her reactions were a bit dramatic, but now I realize how well Mom handled herself.

I've even tried praying. Sometimes I think it helps. I still hurt, but I don't feel as frantic.

I'm pleased you've met someone you care about.

Love, Char

P. S. What do you mean by divine purpose?

Dear Char,

This God stuff is all new to me, but perhaps God can use even your broken heart for some divine design. Remember the summer I broke my arm playing baseball, and the doctor told us that when my arm healed the bone would be stronger than before? I'm thinking that could be true of your heart.

I'm meeting Cyndi at the waterfall for a picnic today.

Love, JW

Dear JW,

The pictures arrived. Cyndi is a doll, but who is that wild man with all that facial hair standing next to her? Surely, Ramboni, a stream is near enough that you could shave. I'm surprised you haven't scared her off. I'm overnighting a shaving kit.

Char shared that you are on a spiritual quest. What a relief. My prayer group has been praying for you for three years. I so want my family to experience Christ's love. Char, too, is seeking answers, although reluctantly. She is reaching out to the God who has been eagerly waiting for her to turn to Him.

Love, Ella

Dear Ella,

I was moved to read that you have prayed for me for so long. Why didn't you tell me? Never mind; I realize I wasn't ready to hear, especially from my big sister. You've been almost like a mom to me—you know, bossy. Don't take that wrong. I appreciate your determination to get us all to do the right thing, but I was wondering if maybe now that we're adults we shouldn't have a real brother-sister relationship. You try not to boss me, and I'll try not to harass you. Deal?

Have you prayed with Char? I think that might help her. Cyndi has been praying with me, and I feel more settled. How interesting that God would use me to save Cyndi and her family from drowning that they might, in turn, save me from my empty existence.

Love, JW

P. S. Yes, I shaved.

Dear JW,

Ella came by last week, and we prayed together. It felt strange yet somehow sweet. I'm not sure how I feel about God or how He feels about me. If  He's going to heal my broken heart, He doesn't seem to be in a hurry. I promise you I am.

My life has taken a dramatic shift with John's leaving, and I have felt so betrayed and alone. But I'm beginning to see a flicker of light on the path ahead. Recently my nights have grown shorter and my days a little fuller. Maybe you were right, big brother. Maybe, somehow, this will work out.

Love, Char

To Ella and Char,

You are invited to the wedding of Jehosophat Willerd Wicket III and Cyndi Rachel Linden. They will, on the third day of October, commit their love and lives to each other under the banner of God's love.

The wedding will take place next to Thunder Falls on Rifle River in canoes (bring life jackets). The Rev. James Linden, the bride's father, will officiate...from land.

Refreshments will follow the service under the falls (bring galoshes).

Proper attire: jeans, hiking boots, sweatshirts, and bowling parkas.

Enclosed is a map (bring compass).

With love, Jehosophat

Dearest JW & Cyndi,
    Pythons couldn't keep us away!

Love, Ella & Char

CLOISTERED

$\mathcal{M}$y heart raced and my head throbbed as footsteps drew closer and closer to my door. I listened to the jingle of keys, and then I heard the apartment door across the hall open and finally close. I took a breath and realized I had broken out in a drenching sweat. I made my way to the kitchen sink, my hands trembling as I turned on the faucet to get a drink to soothe my constricted throat.

Would this madness never end? Year after year afraid of every passing noise. Isolated except from my fear—and it a nagging, jeering roommate. How long could my heart handle this radical racing? It filled my ears with pounding until I wanted to scream. But I must not, I told myself, lest someone come to my aid and find me in this piteous condition. I could hardly bear myself; others should not have to.

How did I, Betty MacKenzie, once the school's Teacher of the Year, end up a prisoner of my own phantom fears? Yes, I'm sane enough to understand my fears are absurd. Yet I'm also insane enough to go to any length to support them. Last week I even placed small pieces of masking tape on the creaky areas of my floor so that I might walk about undetected by those who live below and beside me. It's of utmost importance that people leave me alone. I no longer have anything to say that would make sense to anyone. My thoughts are muddled. My heart is tight. My nerves are tensed.

Tomorrow the deliveryman from the grocery store comes, and I feel the dread of his arrival grow with every passing hour. The first of each month I must go through the torture of opening my door and risking being seen by my neighbors. I have lived in this apartment for three years with all the shades and curtains pulled. Three terrorizing years. And in all that time I have only seen one person, but he did not see me.

About nine months ago, in the wee hours of the morning while others slept, I was taking out the garbage. Suddenly a policeman walked into the alley behind our building. He shone his flashlight into an abandoned car just five feet away from where I stood. I cowered in the shadows, frozen in fear as I clutched my trash. When he walked away, I dropped the plastic bag and, in a panic, fled back inside.

From then on I devised other ways to rid myself of garbage. I finally resorted to writing a letter to my grocery man. I proposed that I leave my garbage outside my door on his delivery day. Then he could drop off my groceries, dispose of my trash, and I would pay him for his services. I insisted, though, that he continue to bring my delivery at 10:00 A.M. sharp because I knew most of the building was empty then.

I slept fitfully that night as my apprehension grew. Finally, tired of wrestling my fear, I dragged myself into the bathroom where I took an aspirin in hopes it would ease my aches, even though I knew they were more from the heart than anywhere else.

I had covered all the mirrors in the apartment several years ago with tablecloths. My haunting reflection had added to my misery, so I had erased it. The reflection may have left, but my misery did not. I washed my hands more often than was needed, I brushed my teeth until my gums bled, and I gargled until my neck ached from tilting my head back. I was down to three mended outfits that I rotated. My sister had left me her wardrobe—and her savings—but I felt sad whenever I saw her things. I'd rather go without than add to my anguish.

In the morning, which came before I managed to get much sleep, I wore my striped cotton house smock. It snapped down the front and had two generous pockets that had become tattered at the edges. I carried my medication in one pocket and my mom's Bible in the other. Neither comforted me, but habit demanded I have them near. Actually, I had only three tranquilizers left. I was saving them for extreme emergencies. The doctor's office said I couldn't have any more refills unless I went to the office for a checkup. What would I do?

I waited until 9:45 to set out my trash lest a neighbor complain to the landlord that my garbage was littering the hall. As I headed to the door, I felt dizzy and feared I might pass out. My chest began to tighten as I fought for each breath. I leaned against the wall and closed my eyes. Finally, in one motion I drew in my breath, opened the door, and pushed the bag into the hall. Just as I turned to step back inside, the door across the hall jerked open and an elderly woman called out, "Good morning."

I felt like a deer caught in a headlight. I was transfixed, looking straight at her. Our eyes met, and then my instincts kicked in, and I bolted for the safety of my home, locking the door behind me. My worst fear had come upon me. My mind raced, my heart was in my throat, and I felt nauseous. I reached down into my pocket and grasped the bottle of tranquilizers. I fumbled with it, and the bottle fell to the floor and rolled under the couch. I dropped to my knees to retrieve it, but when I slid my arm under the couch, my fingers touched the container, and it rolled farther away. As I knelt forward, my face brushed the cushion. The softness of it startled me, and I began to sob. The deep sounds, which I muffled in the cushion, frightened me as they poured out, until I was left weakened and still.

I stayed on the floor next to the couch, limp from the convulsive crying. I had not cried in years. Then I realized it was one o'clock, and my groceries were still sitting outside my door. If I didn't get them soon, my surrounding neighbors would return from their jobs, and the halls would be filled with people.

An idea came to me, and I hurried into my narrow bedroom, pulled two hangers out of the closet, and began to unwind them. Then I twisted them together and formed a hook at one end. I tiptoed to my door and listened for footsteps. There were none, so I quietly unlocked and opened the door several inches, staying hidden behind it. I dangled my extended hook toward the groceries, snagged the corner of the box, and inched it toward me. When it was close enough to take hold of, I dragged it in and closed my door.

After I carried the groceries into the kitchen, all I wanted to do was sleep. I was depleted. This had been a horrific day. But first I had to put away my food. It wouldn't take long, though, because I was eating less and less, which was just as well. Less food, less garbage. I carefully cleaned off each can with disinfectant before lining it up with the others on the shelves. As I pulled a box of rice out of one of the bags, an envelope fell to the floor. I couldn't imagine why the grocer would bill me when I always paid in advance by mail. I picked it up. Already, with just the threat of communication, my hands were perspiring.

The note inside read,

> I am so sorry I startled you. I am your neighbor, Mrs. Bradley. I wanted to extend a hand of friendship to you. Forgive my awkward start. Might we have tea sometime? At your convenience please.
>
> Mrs. Bradley
> (Psalm 18:2)

I dropped the card, went into the bedroom, and threw myself across the bed. My head was swimming with the day's confusion. I tried to slow down my thoughts, and eventually I drifted off into a restless dream in which Mrs. Bradley was chasing me down the hall carrying my garbage. She kept telling the neighbors to look out their doors to see what kind of woman I was. Then a police officer shone his flashlight in my eyes while Mrs. Bradley read verses from the Bible.

I awoke with a start and realized it was dark outside, and I was having a nightmare. *No, I am living a nightmare.*

The next day I reread Mrs. Bradley's note. Who was she anyway? I knew she hadn't lived there more than three months because I'd listened at my door the day she moved in. I didn't know why she had to bother me. She was probably some meddling old woman with nothing better to do than agitate others.

Before the day was over, out of curiosity, I looked up the verse at the bottom of her note. It read, "The LORD is my rock and my fortress and my deliverer, my God, my rock, in whom I take refuge; my shield and the horn of my salvation, my stronghold."

Why had she put that verse on the note? I read it over and over. I'm not certain why, but I did. Sometimes I read it and felt anger toward her. The next time I felt confusion. Over the following few days I read the verse so often that I knew it by heart.

I believed in God, but I felt forsaken by Him. For if He loved me, why hadn't He rescued me from the emotional anguish I was in? Why hadn't He stopped the terror, the panic? Why hadn't God been my deliverer?

Several days later I heard Mrs. Bradley at her door fumbling for her keys. She was singing. The words she sang I hadn't heard in years.

"Turn your eyes upon Jesus, look full in His wonderful face…"

I wondered if she knew I was listening?

"and the cares of earth will grow strangely dim…"

Her voice was sweet and gentle.

"in the light of His glory and grace."

Mrs. Bradley's door opened and closed, and then the song was gone. As I leaned against the doorframe, I realized a stream of tears had dampened my face. Where were these tears coming from? I didn't want to feel anything; I didn't want to remember. I just wanted to be left alone.

Mrs. Bradley's song hung in my mind like haunting moss in an oak tree. "Turn your eyes upon Jesus…" I couldn't even face my neighbor; how could I look at God?

The following week I heard Mrs. Bradley's door open, but I didn't hear her walk away. My heart began to pound. I stared at my door, fearful she would knock. Then I saw a note being inched underneath. Finally her footsteps carried the threat of invasion away from me. I didn't touch the note for several hours until something within me gave in, and I picked it up.

The fragrance of lilacs wafted up from the note. Lilacs. I hadn't smelled lilacs in years. A nine-year-old red-headed student named Timmy Watson presented me with an armload of purple lilacs when I taught at the Grapevine Elementary School. I had been pleased with such a fragrant offering. Later that day an irate neighbor next to the school came over to complain that some imp of a boy had decimated her lilac bush.

The memory made me smile. What an odd sensation...to smile. I pressed my hand to my mouth to verify it. Why, yes, it was a smile.

Turning back the fold of paper, I slowly read Mrs. Bradley's note.

Dear Neighbor, today during my prayer time I thought of you. I hope your day is pleasant. Perhaps soon we could have our cup of tea. If you need anything, please let me know. I'd like to be a friend.

Mrs. Bradley
(Psalm 27:1)

I reached for my Bible and read her verse. "The LORD is my light and my salvation; whom shall I fear? The LORD is the defense of my life; whom shall I dread?"

Over the next few months the notes appeared several times. Always short and always with a Bible verse. Once, when I snagged my groceries with my hook and hauled them in, a small extra bag contained some home-made brownies from Mrs. Bradley. The aroma was heartwarming, but I didn't eat them. Instead I smelled them until they were stale and their aroma had faded away. Another time a small bouquet of pansies appeared huddled in the corner of a grocery sack with a note that read,

May these flowers add sweetness to your day.

Mrs. B.
(Genesis 1:1)

I had eight notes from Mrs. B. that I kept tucked in my pocket with my Bible. At first I wasn't going to keep them, but I did. Sometimes when I couldn't sleep, I would pull them out and reread them. My neighbor puzzled me. Why would she bother with someone she didn't know—and someone who never responded to her attempts at friendship?

I often dozed in the afternoon in my brown tweed upholstered rocking chair, which was once my mother's. Mom napped in the chair every day at three. Sitting in it made me feel closer to her.

Recently I had taken to lifting the shade just a little to allow a sliver of sunlight in to warm me. The playfulness of the light dancing about my hand would lull me to sleep.

One naptime I dreamed of fields of flowers calling my name and a little red-headed boy who smelled like brownies and giggled as he dashed about the field. Then the flowers turned to jeering people chasing after the boy. I awoke angry. I felt protective of that carefree child. Why didn't they leave him alone? I paced the floor, and then I did the strangest thing. I ripped all the masking tape off the floor, wadded it up, and threw it away.

That week two more notes arrived, but the handwriting looked shaky or forced. Still, the notes were cheerful. Maybe I was imagining the change. She looked well enough.

I knew this because a month earlier I had removed the many layers of tape I had used to seal the peephole, leaving one loosely attached strip for my privacy. When I heard Mrs. B.'s footsteps approach her door, I would lift the tape and watch her enter her apartment. I didn't mean to spy. I just wanted a better look at the woman. She appeared to be in her midseventies, stylishly dressed, and quite spry.

Grocery day came around again. Before I pulled out my cans of food, I looked in the bags to see if Mrs. B. had sent me something. Nestled among the cans was a floral package with a mauve ribbon wrapped around it. The tag read, "To my neighbor, to my friend."

I sat and stared at the gift for the longest time. A present for me. How long had it been since someone had given me a wrapped gift? Oh yes, my sister, Hannah, gave me a diamond stickpin. Hannah died eight years ago, soon after our mom's death.

Had it really been eight years since I lost Hannah and Mom, since my life had unraveled? A dull ache filled my being.

First Daddy, the delight of my life, died when I was eight. I suffered terribly after that with headaches and nightmares. But Mom, Hannah, and I promised always to be there for each other. I was the delicate one. Mom and Hannah knew that, and they helped me cope even as an adult. Then Mom had a heart attack and died. Two months later Hannah fell on the front steps and struck her head on a rock. She was in a coma for three days, and then she, too, left me, left me all alone.

My mind circled back to Mrs. B.'s present. I picked up the package and moved out of the kitchen. Sitting down in my rocker, I placed the gift in my lap. I rocked for several hours before I unwrapped it. I carefully removed the paper and opened the top of the box to find an exquisite yellow teacup with purple violets, some assorted tea bags, and, of course, a note.

> This cup is from a tea set that belonged to my mother. I drink
> from a cup just like it at six every evening. Perhaps you, too,
> could pour yourself some tea at the same time and we could
> think of each other.
>
> Mrs. B.

Tears spilled off my cheek and dripped right into the teacup. I didn't know what to think of Mrs. Bradley's generous gesture. And she called me "friend." I wondered if someday we could be friends?

Oh, what a foolish thought. If she saw me, she would change her mind.

Placing the cup on the kitchen counter, I walked into the bathroom. I hesitated a moment, and then I pulled back the cloth covering the bathroom mirror. My hair was grayer than I remembered. I had it tightly secured in the back. It looked severe. My face was thin, and my colorless skin caused me to look anemic. I also looked much older than my forty-eight years. I picked up a brush and began to run it through my hair. Then I found an old bottle of foundation at the bottom of a drawer, and I dabbed some on in an attempt to smooth out the look of my skin. I rustled around in some old purses until I located two tubes of lipstick. One tube was melted, but the other was usable. I rubbed a little on my cheeks and ran the color over my lips. I looked unnatural. I grabbed some tissue and rubbed off the color. I looked at my clock. It was almost six, so I hurried to the kitchen.

I sat down at the table with my tea and thought about Mrs. B. I spread all her notes on the table and reread each one. That's when I noticed that her last card didn't have a verse. That dismayed me. It was so unlike her. I felt uneasy, so I finished my tea and headed for my rocker.

I couldn't rock my neighbor off my mind. I thought of all her kindnesses and how I had come to depend on her to fill my day—her footsteps, her singing, her notes—and I had given nothing in return.

In the night, while the building slept, I knelt down and pulled a blanket box from under my bed. Digging beneath the folded quilts, I unearthed a tin box. I sat on the edge of the bed and pried off the lid. Inside were items I hadn't looked at since I had moved to my apartment: pictures, a locket, my teacher's certificate, three death certificates, three wills, some stationery, and an assortment of note cards.

I chose a card with a robin perched on a tree branch singing. I wasn't certain what I would write. After an hour I settled on the words, "Thank you." But how should I sign it? Apt. 12B? Ms. MacKenzie? Betty? Nothing seemed appropriate. Finally I decided on "your neighbor." I wanted to say "friend," but I couldn't bring myself to take that kind of risk.

I started to seal the envelope but then stopped, reached in my pocket, and pulled out my Bible. I added, "Philippians 1:3."

I leaned against my door and listened for movement, then I peeked through the viewer. The hall was empty, and the building was quiet. I slowly opened the door and looked again in each direction. My heart fluttered, and my hands shook as I tiptoed across the hall and slid the card under Mrs. B.'s door. As I turned to hurry back to my apartment, I tripped over her door-mat and went stumbling across the hall and into my living room. Steadying myself, I jerked the door closed and flipped the lock.

Then something happened I can't explain. Whether it was my nerves or the excitement or the fact I tripped, I don't know, but I started to laugh. And I laughed and laughed until tears ran down my face, and my nose started to run. I felt like a child who had just left a surprise package under the Christmas tree for her mom.

A short time later I climbed into bed, and as I drifted off to sleep, I whispered, "God bless Mrs. B."

The next day I watched my floor for a return note, but none came. Nor did I hear from her the following day. What a mistake. I shouldn't have answered her. She didn't really want to be friends. My thoughts began to gang up on me, defending Mrs. B. one moment and condemning her and myself the next. My head throbbed with tension. I took two aspirin and sat down in my rocker.

Then I heard a door open. I rushed to my viewer and saw Mrs. B. lock her door. Then she grabbed the doorframe as if to steady herself, and she slumped to the floor. Before I thought, I was out my door and at her side. I took her hand and began to pat it. She looked so pale. I ran back into my apartment, wet a washcloth, and grabbed an ice tray from my freezer. I placed the compress on her head and touched her temples gently with the ice. She stirred and then opened her eyes.

"Oh my, what have I gone and done? My dear," she said looking up at me, "how kind of you to help."

I assisted her to a sitting position, and then I scurried to get her a drink of water. She told me she had not felt well for several days and was on her way to the doctor's when she fainted.

After she felt strong enough to stand, I held her arm while she unlocked her door. Mrs. B. was going to call her son to come and drive her to her appointment. "Will you stay with me until he arrives?" she asked me gently.

She must have wondered if I was mute, for I hadn't spoken one word. At her request, I heard myself say, "I will try."

How odd that must have sounded to her, but she acted as if that was the right thing to say. She smiled and thanked me for trying. For some reason I had the feeling Mrs. B. understood my struggles better than I did, which made me feel safe with her.

"Why don't I put on some tea for us?" she said.

"Oh, I couldn't do that yet," I answered, catching my breath at the very thought.

She nodded to let me know that was all right. Her door was ajar, as was mine, and Mrs. B. seemed to understand that was important to me. After twenty minutes had passed, I heard footsteps in the hall, and my heart began to stampede. My eyes darted in her direction, and she said, "Why don't you go now. I'll be fine. Thank you again. You've been a true friend."

I didn't answer but instead dashed to the safety of my own place, never looking in the direction of her son, and quickly closed the door behind me. I heard Mrs. B.'s and her son's muffled voices, and then I heard them leave.

Several hours later they returned. I wanted so to know what had happened, but I kept myself busy tidying up my living room. It had been awhile since I had moved the furniture to dust. When I tried to swing one end of my tan couch out from the wall, I noticed a note had been slid under my door. I opened it and read,

The doctor has decided that I need a series of B_{12} shots to help combat my aging blood count. I'm not anemic, and they don't want me to be. Rest and vitamins, and I should be fit as a fiddle. Again, thank you for coming to my rescue. Would you mind if

I come over this evening at six with my teacup, and we have tea before I retire? If this is not acceptable, just slide a note under my door.

Mrs. B.

Proverbs 17:17

Let her in my apartment? No. I wasn't ready for that. I grabbed the tin box off my dresser and pulled out a blank note card.

Mrs. B., tonight would not be a good time for me.

Ms. MacKenzie

I listened at my door. The hall was still. I opened the door so I could deliver my reply. I started to step out when I heard children running and laughing in a distant hall. I held back and listened. One child called out to the other as he ran, "I'm going to hide. Bet you can't find me."

I closed my door and slid to the floor. "Oh, God, please find me. Be my Deliverer. Rescue me from the stronghold of fear and teach me what it means to make You my refuge." Tears coursed down my face, and something inside me shifted. I wasn't certain what changed, but I knew I didn't feel the same. I took the note and tore it up. Then I brought some order to my surroundings. Near the appointed hour, I set out my yellow teacup and put on the kettle. At six o'clock Mrs. B. gently tapped on my door…and…I opened it.

What a Blessing

The community of Blessing seemed to be exactly that for its citizens. When passersby dropped in or breezed through Blessing, they would promise themselves that one day they, too, would live in a town far from the city's stark realities. A place where waiting in lines was rare and the only traffic jams were when Marabelle Sater forgot to take her car out of gear, causing it to drift onto Badger Street. One time her '72 Buick sat in the middle of the street for two hours before anyone noticed.

Crime was low in Blessing and usually consisted of childish pranks. Like the time little Tommy Volt poured a box of popcorn kernels down the fire station's chimney. The kernels started exploding like tiny grenades just as the tottering Chief dozed off in his easy chair. Thinking Blessing had come under enemy attack, he hit the community alert system, and ten armed volunteers arrived before he crawled out from under Engine No. 7 and discovered a profusion of puffy yellow corn scattered throughout the firehouse.

Tommy might have gotten away with his antic, but when the Chief did a lineup of the neighborhood kids, Tommy couldn't quit laughing, and on close inspection corn kernels were found dangling in his britches' cuffs.

The young lad all but lost his sense of humor when every Saturday for a month the Chief had Tommy scrub down the fire station.

Although crime was unusual in Blessing, living within the town limits was the notorious Mrs. Webster, whose criminal actions were known throughout the county. She had a rap list as long as your arm for lambasting her husband, Ned, with her genuine Teflon-coated skillet. But hers was a fairly predictable crime since it always coincided with her Bingo losses. Bingo games were held in Blessing's City Hall the third Tuesday of the month. If Mrs. Webster, better known to most folks as B-9, won, all was well at the homestead. But if B-9 didn't get to leap up and yell her favorite five-letter word, old Ned was sure to get a beaning before the night was over. He had more knots on his head than a Bingo card had numbers. Many wondered why Lumpy stayed with the missis, but consensus was she had knocked him plumb silly before he had the good sense God gave a goose to skedaddle.

Most of Blessing's citizens were temperate people who owned a car (of questionable vintage), a dog, cat, or bird, and who attended church (except on holidays and during hunting, fishing, and harvest season). Blessing was in a dry county, which may account for the goodwill lifestyle of the community at large. That and, of course, Miss Lorna.

Miss Lorna was an odd one. She wasn't exactly a recluse because she was often seen out and about, lurking in the shadows. There's just something about a looming, red-headed, sunglasses-adorned, bulky woman that looks suspicious. She always dressed in layers, often using discarded clothes that she would pull right out of someone's trash. Sometimes she would sport a dozen layers of assorted colors and sizes, not to mention stripes and prints. Draped around Lorna's neck was her hallmark accessory, a lime green wool scarf. In the dead of winter or the scorching heat of summer, the scarf was a constant in her eclectic wardrobe.

Lorna lived in a trailer next to the railroad tracks, and every time a train would pass, she would run out to wave. The engineer on the afternoon run would sound one long whistle to acknowledge her, and it got so folks could set their watches by the 3:15 wave. That appeared to be the extent of her social life, and some believed that daily afternoon tryst was the closest she had ever come to a date.

People in the area would have liked to outlaw Lorna, but she wasn't doing anything wrong except getting on Blessing's last nerve. The founding fathers were concerned with protecting the community's reputation as the state's fifteenth largest tobacco grower. But Lorna's outlandish behavior was, in many citizens' opinion, a smudge on Blessing's sterling character. She didn't dress like them, socialize like them, or worship like them.

Mrs. Webster told Ned once, "I saw Loony Lorna out in a field dancing in the rain and heard her shouting to the Lord, like He was hard of hearing or something. They need to lock that woman up." Ned nodded. (Poor Ned often looked like one of those bobbing-head animals that folks set in their car's back window.)

Marabelle Sater watched from her kitchen window one summer morning as Lorna rifled through Marabelle's donation bags she had set out for the Salvation Army. Lorna held up Marabelle's discarded clothing as if she were shopping at the local dress shop. Finally, Marabelle rapped on her window, and Lorna, startled, ran off, dragging Marabelle's rumpled housecoat with her. Marabelle considered calling the police, but she had an outstanding ticket and decided she didn't want to get involved filling out a report.

Story has it that during the town's annual Tobacco Parade, Lorna was seen perched atop the water tower, lime green scarf flapping in the breeze, as she watched the festivities through binoculars. Mrs. Webster spotted her and nudged Ned. "What a snoop! She ought to be arrested." Ned, of course, nodded.

After the celebration the Fire Chief caught sight of Lorna as she picked up a fallen parade flag, placed it under her arm, and scurried for home. He thought about turning the fire hose on that "little pack rat," but he was plumb tuckered out from all the waving during the parade, so he just let her go. Besides, the parade committee already had decided to toss out the festive flags since they were tattered from years of use.

About a week later an explosion shook Blessing right down to its tobacco plants' roots. Lorna's thirty-five-foot trailer blew up, with pieces skyrocketing hundreds of feet in the air and falling in all directions. It seems her home had an undetected gas leak, and when the afternoon train passed by, a spark from the caboose lit the grass, which in turn ignited the gas.

Much to the feigned dismay of Blessing's citizens, Lorna could not be located. Some figured she had been blown to kingdom come, while others presumed she was nearby rooting around in someone's trash.

The following day the postal worker delivered a bulky package to City Hall addressed to "The Good Folks of Blessing." The return address read in large print, "From Lorna with love."

An emergency community meeting was called, and all of Blessing assembled that evening for the opening of the mysterious package. The Fire Chief, being Blessing's oldest resident, was designated the official opener.

At the appointed moment, the Chief carefully untied the twine and pulled back the paper to expose a beautifully crafted quilt. Puzzled, he shook out the quilt to its king size as the town looked on in amazement. There before their eyes was a visual record of the community. Every event over the past twenty-five years was represented by a square of cloth titled in beautiful needlepoint. Around the quilt's perimeter was a square for every Blessing resident, with each person's name carefully stitched in the appropriate square.

"Well I swanie," announced Marabelle Sater. "My square is made from my old housecoat."

"Yes, and them's my popcorn britches in my square," little Tommy Volt confessed.

"Look, Ned," Mrs. Webster said, as she poked her hubby in the ribs with her elbow, "mine is designed to look like a Bingo card. And yours… hmm, looks like a skillet."

"Why, that's the material from the parade flag used as a background for the city council members' names," the Chief observed aloud, scratching his head.

"Hey, Jeb, isn't that a piece off your old awning from the drugstore?" Marabelle asked.

"Yep, and that purple square representing the church is from the communion cloth we replaced a few years ago when I was on the committee."

Marabelle's seamstress neighbor said, "This must have taken her years to create. It's flawless."

Slowly the impact of this exquisite work settled on the people, and a hush fell over the room.

Mrs. Webster broke the quiet when she proclaimed, "I always said there was something special about that woman, didn't I, Ned?"

Ned nodded.

By the end of the week, when there still was no sign of Lorna, she officially was declared deceased. Her gift to the community was hung under glass in City Hall, and a fund-raiser was held to erect a statue in the park in Lorna's memory. The community chose to depict her in her sunglasses, dressed in layers, waving enthusiastically at the train.

However, since the explosion, Blessing's residents have noted that, when the 3:15 train passes by, streaming off the back of the caboose is a long, lime green article of clothing.

STARDUST

$\mathcal{W}$*hat was all that clatter? I headed for the front window of our home just as a big moving truck clanked past the house, followed closely, like a duckling after its mom, by a smaller U-Haul rental truck. In the front seat bobbed a young girl's head as she gazed out. In that instant I was flooded with memories of a move I had made when I was wide-eyed and young...*

Melancholy rinsed over my ten-year-old soul as we backed the U-Haul truck into the driveway of our new home. New? Hardly. Several of the black shutters on the windows hung askew, one side of the porch railing was missing, and the storm-door window was cracked. If rickety wasn't bad enough, the forty-year-old structure had the unmistakable contours of a barn.

In the past Mom had scolded me and my seven-year-old brother, Jake, because our respective rooms looked as though animals inhabited them, but I didn't think we deserved this. And the previous owners, as if they were proud of this farmyard building, had painted it red—barn red. I, Judy Banks, whose favorite color was beige, was about to be humiliated daily by my new habitat.

Jake was ecstatic—he who wore his Davy Crockett headgear to bed and who received the Golden Pickle Award from the Boys Banshee Club in our old neighborhood for burping the loudest and the longest. Of course Jake would think a building for livestock was a good place to call home.

I inched my way inside the building, fearing I might have to face a trough in the kitchen or find I would be bedded down in a stall. But the inside resembled a real house. That is, with the exception of my bedroom. I was mortified when I found my room contained a loft where my bed was located.

Jake begged to change rooms with me, but Mom said it was out of the question because of his midnight sleepwalking escapades. I gladly would have given up this peculiar arrangement. I couldn't imagine scaling a ladder to go to bed.

The door to the room was odd, too. It was cut in half like you might find in a barn. For a moment I imagined my mother flinging open the top half to toss in bales of hay for my breakfast.

After our initial exploration of the house, Jake and I spent the next three hours helping to haul in labeled boxes and deposit them in the appropriate rooms. Then Mom ran out to buy us White Castle hamburgers while Jake and I stayed at the house to watch for Grandpa Frank, who was to arrive with a truckload of more of our worldly goods.

Jake rummaged around until he found his bike and rode up and down our driveway, singing at the top of his voice, "Davy Crockett, King of the Wild Frontier." I headed for the backyard lest someone in the neighborhood think I was related to him. Or worse yet, try to talk to me. I wasn't ready to admit this was where I lived.

The fenced backyard was full of maple trees, blue spruce, lilac bushes, and one huge oak tree. The oak looked tired from years of holding up its own weight. I knew how it felt, so I headed for its shelter. Exhausted, I sat down and leaned against the oak's trunk to consider my plight. Tears rushed into my eyes.

Then a tiny voice broke into my privacy. "Excuse me. Excuse me please."

I jumped up, startled that words were coming from the branches above me.

Again the voice spoke, "Could you please help me?"

I followed the sound to a nearby spruce tree where, about seven feet up, I spotted an elfish girl's face peering down through the needles.

"I seem to have traveled past my point of comfort and will need some assistance in getting down. Would you happen to have a ladder?" she inquired.

I started to ask the young stranger what she was doing in our tree, but she requested I hurry because the pine needles were quite unpleasant. In spite of my fresh tears, I giggled at this sprite of a girl and her odd way of talking as I ran to the garage to grab the ladder. Quickly I dragged it into the yard.

After several tries I steadied it against the branches near the tree urchin. She carefully boarded the ladder and made her way down.

"Well, now," she said as she brushed off her clothing, "that is what one gets when one tries to peek in the new kid's window!"

I laughed. She chortled too. We couldn't stop giggling until we folded over with aches in our sides.

Her thin arms were covered in red streaks from the pine boughs, black pine pitch dappled her clothing, and she had a pine cone snarled in her chestnut hair. I helped to extricate the pine needles from her hands and arms, disentangled the cone from her hair, and brought her a warm wash-cloth from the house to help scrub off the pitch.

"My name's Suzanne. What's yours?" She stuck her hand out for us to shake.

I stared at the hand a moment, surprised by this adult gesture. Then I put my hand into her little one and simply said, "Judy."

"Everyone calls me Dinky," she went on. "That's because I'm so petite. But I'm eleven—I know I don't look it. How old are you?"

I felt small myself since I had neither a nickname to offer nor any colorful description of myself. "Ten."

"Great! Well, welcome to the neighborhood. I'm sure we'll be seeing lots of each other since I live three doors down. Next time I come over, I'll ring the doorbell instead of climbing your tree." With a giggle and good-bye wave, Dinky scampered out of my yard.

That night, when I climbed into my loft, I thought of Dinky's disruptive arrival into my life, and I fell asleep smiling. I had a new friend.

And Dinky did show up—the next day. She decided to introduce me to the neighborhood so we hopped on our bikes and started to wheel down the road.

"You live in the best house on the street," Dinky announced.

"Really? Don't you think it's too red and, well, like a barn?"

"Anyone can live in a box-shaped house, but only the fortunate live in a barn-shaped dwelling."

I looked at the various box-shaped houses we were pedaling past. And a funny thing happened. I found I didn't mind the shape of our house anymore.

"C'mon," Dinky called to me as she propped up her bicycle in front of a little market with a sign above the door that read, "Mrs. Pritchard's Grocery Mart."

As I neared the bicycle rack, in one fell swoop I hit the brakes, swung my leg over the seat, and put down the kickstand. I could tell Dinky was impressed.

"Way to ride, Hopalong Judy," Dinky teased, as she swung the door wide and entered the store.

"Hello, Dinky," a high-pitched voice called from behind the cash register. We turned to see a white-haired, tall woman who was as narrow as a drinking straw.

"Hello, Mrs. Pritchard," Dinky responded in a voice that sounded loud in the small store.

"Remember, Dinky, no sampling the produce," Mrs. Pritchard instructed as she adjusted her wire-rimmed glasses. "Rumpled produce is not attractive," she added, scrunching up her nose to show her displeasure.

"No ma'am. I mean, yes ma'am," Dinky said. I could tell by the look on her face she was trying to swallow a giggle. She grabbed my hand and headed for the freezer section, where Popsicles and a nice variety of ice cream treats waited for us. We snickered as we discussed our selections and then handed over our money to Mrs. Pritchard, who never seemed to take her eyes off us. After we left the store, we tittered all the way home about Mrs. Pritchard and her rumpled fruit.

One night shortly after that, Mom said Dinky could sleep over. We lined a basket with dishtowels and filled it with popcorn for Mom, Jake, Dinky, and me. Then, after endless hours of playing Monopoly, Dinky and I moved into my bedroom.

As we slipped into our p.j.'s, Dinky said, "Judy, where's your dad? I've never seen him."

I gulped down the lump in my throat and pretended I was having a hard time with the top button on my pajamas. "He's away," I finally said.

Dinky was quiet for a while, but I didn't dare look at her.

"Hey, getting into bed is going to be fun," she said as she climbed the ladder into the loft.

I followed her and found, when I reached the loft, Dinky was gazing at the view of the evening sky out my window. Then, turning toward my bed, she pointed and said, "Look at the stardust, Judy."

I turned and there, on my pillow, was a pool of moonlight. It was filtered through the screen on the window, making the light look like golden stardust.

"If you sleep on a pillow covered in stardust," she whispered, "you'll get to peek in heaven's window in your dreams and maybe even see an angel."

I leaned back into my stardusty pillow and soon fell sound asleep. I didn't dream of heaven, but I didn't mind. Just the thought of it was pleasant.

The next morning being Sunday, Dinky asked me if I could attend church with her. Of course I wanted to be with Dinky, but church? What if I was asked to do something, and I wouldn't know how to do it? Dinky promised me she would stick with me and I wouldn't have to do anything hard. So off we went.

Dinky's church contained beautiful stained-glass windows, joyous music, and green hymnals full of heart-cheering words. The rest of the summer I never missed a service.

A few weeks later, Dinky and I decided to pick strawberries for tarts to take to the upcoming church picnic. As we collected the plump red fruit jewels, the warmth of the sun and the warmth of the love I felt for Dinky overtook me with happiness. "Dinky, am I your best friend?"

"No," Dinky answered and kept picking strawberries. Then she glanced up and must have seen the pain on my face. "Jesus is my first best friend," she quickly added. "And you're my next best friend."

Dinky's answer made my stomach knot and my throat ache. We plucked strawberries in silence after that.

In time I made peace with Dinky's response. What else could I do? I certainly didn't want to lose this magenta friend from my beige world.

And she did add color to my life. Like the day she added black and blue by introducing me to horseback riding. We started off okay, but then Dinky's horse turned unexpectedly and trotted back to the barn.

"Hey, stop!" Dinky commanded, pulling on the reins. Her actions seemed to spur on the horse, and he began to run pell-mell. My horse followed, and I went along for the ride.

When the horse and I entered the barn, Dinky was on her head in a haystack where the horse had deposited her. He was standing in his stall looking triumphant.

"Now you just stop that kind of behavior, Mr. Smarty-Pants," Dinky lectured the horse after she had righted herself. "We're going for a ride, and that's it." Then, without hesitation, she pounced onto the horse's back. He seemed to get the message and behaved ever so nicely after that.

I, on the other hand, still had several novice challenges awaiting me. The biggest was staying in the saddle, which I kept tumbling out of.

"You can do it, Judy," Dinky encouraged me after each fall. "That horse just needs to figure out who's boss."

With her encouraging words echoing in my ears, I'd shake off the dust and reboard the horse, whom we chose to call Eeyore for his stubborn ways.

Finally I seemed to be getting the hang of it—or was it that Eeyore figured out I was boss?

"Ride 'em, Cowgirl!" Dinky called out to me, as Mr. Smarty-Pants moved into a trot. Eeyore followed, and I clung on.

While I bobbed up and down and tried to stay upright, I saw Dinky's horse turn toward a grove of trees, and I pulled the reins in that direction. Miraculously, Eeyore obeyed.

But the next thing I knew, a herd of irate yellow jackets was swarming around Eeyore and me. I felt stings on my face and arms. Eeyore had stopped moving forward and was snorting, his eyes wild, and his tail flicking angrily.

"Dismount, Judy! Hurry!" I heard Dinky call to me.

Her voice was so commanding that I obeyed. The next thing I knew, Dinky was standing beside me, swatting away the insects and holding Eeyore's reins.

"Let's get out of here," she said, leading Eeyore, Mr. Smarty-Pants, and me out of the yellow jackets' territory.

"Eeyore must have stepped on the yellow jackets' nest," Judy speculated as we walked back to the nurse's station. "And they sent out a posse to protest."

The cowboy image made me laugh, despite the way my face and arms felt like prickly needles had been stabbed into them.

After the nurse put salve on the bites, Dinky and I ambled off toward home. She had a bruise on her forehead from her tumble in the hay, my legs ached from trying to bend around Eeyore's sides, my backside was thrumming from all my "dismounts," and my arms and face were swollen.

"We'll look back on this day as a wonderful memory," Dinky suddenly announced.

"I don't think so," I said through my swollen lips.

Dinky laughed. "You'll see," she promised.

After we reached home, we settled under the oak tree to recover from our memory-making. As our fingers searched through the tufts of grass for four-leaf clovers, Dinky asked, "When's your dad coming home?"

I couldn't answer. I don't know where my tears came from. I hadn't cried about my dad for months, but the tears soon turned to sobs. Poor Dinky mustn't have known what to do because she tried to make me laugh. That only made me wail louder. In desperation Dinky fell to her knees and began to pray aloud for me. She was almost shouting to be heard over my bellowing. At first I couldn't concentrate on her prayers, but as she held steadfast in her supplications, I began to settle down a bit.

"Oh, Lord," she was saying, "help my friend Judy. It sounds like her heart is broken, and I know you fix broken things. It sounds like you'll need to hurry, though. Thank you for making us friends. Help me to help her. Dry her tears. And Lord—"

"Dinky," I interrupted through my sniffles, "my dad died. He left for work one day, and I never saw him again. He was in a car pileup in the fog on the freeway."

Dinky sat ever so still, as if she would break into a thousand pieces if she dared move, and then she began to cry. I didn't know what to do, and soon I was crying again too.

Dinky grabbed my hand and choked out the words, "Judy, I'm so sorry." Then my tiny friend hugged me, and we both emptied our tears. Afterwards I felt so relieved and so comforted.

A few days later I received a card from Dinky. The envelope was decorated with stickers, and each letter of my name was printed in a different color. The card, which was made from construction paper, had a hand-drawn picture of two friends holding hands looking skyward. Dinky had written, "Remember, Judy, heaven has many daddies waiting for their daughters. Love, Dinky."

I liked that thought a lot. I had never had a friend who cried with me until Dinky.

We didn't see eye to eye on everything, though. Like the time we were going to go to the city pool for a swim and Dinky thought we should invite my brother to go with us.

"Are you crazy? Invite Jake the Flake on purpose? I don't think so!"

Dinky screwed up her little face until she looked like Mrs. Pritchard from the corner store. Then Dinky wagged her finger in my face, instructing me not to touch the produce. By the time she was done mimicking Mrs. P., I was on the floor in gales of giggles.

After the laughter had softened my heart, Dinky reminded me, "Brothers are a gift from the Lord."

"Yes, and He created porcupines, too, but I don't want to take them to the pool. Or skunks!" I added.

"But people aren't animals," she protested. "Besides, Judy, you know better than most that sometimes people leave us. We need to enjoy each other. And Jake is fun!"

Fun? What a thought! My burping, hat-wearing, sleepwalking, annoying brother, fun?

Although one day Mom and I had laughed hard and long when Jake found a bag of clothes we were discarding, and he put on a modeling show for us. And there was the time he chewed up a mouthful of crackers and tried to whistle "She'll Be Comin' 'Round the Mountain." And Jake did do clever imitations of Cecil the Sea Serpent, Red Skelton, and Donald Duck. *Hmm, I guess Jake is kind of fun,* I thought.

We took Jake that day. I wish I had a picture of my mother's face when I announced we wanted him to come with us.

The three of us did cannonballs off the diving board and played water tag. Dinky even climbed up to the highest board and dove in. She was so daring. Then we ate lunch at the hot dog stand and sat on the curb waiting for our food to settle so we could swim again. But Dinky wasn't feeling well, so we went home instead.

The next day I called Dinky to see if she could go to the movies with me, but her mom said Dinky was running a fever and would have to rest. Disappointed for me and sad for her, I moped around the house for the next two days, lost without my friend.

Then on Wednesday the phone rang, and I could tell by my mom's intense look something was wrong. After she hung up the phone, she said, "Honey, Dinky has been taken to the hospital. She's quite ill."

I stared at my mom. Then her words forced their way into my mind like unwanted guests who had come to the door and barged on in. I felt scared.

I wasn't allowed to see Dinky because they said she was too weak for visitors. But I wasn't a visitor; I was her second-best friend. And friends are supposed to help each other when they hurt. Dinky had taught me that.

In church on Sunday the pastor told the congregation that the doctors had discovered Dinky had a congenital heart defect. But he called her Suzanne. I wondered if she would mind. Charlie Watkins, the paperboy, had called her Suzanne once, and she had put a garden snake in his saddlebag.

When we were all supposed to bow our heads to pray for her, I slipped out of the pew and walked home. I made my way into the backyard and sat under the oak tree.

There I bowed my head. "Jesus, please rescue Dinky. And me. Will you be my best friend just like you're Dinky's?" Then I lay down on the grass and cried myself to sleep.

When I woke up, I was wrapped in my mother's arms. Her warm tears fell into my hair as she rocked back and forth. I knew what that meant. I didn't speak for the longest time. Nor did she.

At the funeral Dinky's mom handed me a card Dinky had made for me. I clutched it lovingly, but I didn't open it until I was home and could look at it alone. I went back to the oak tree and sat down. The writing was wobbly, but I could tell it was hers. She had drawn a picture of the spruce tree with two large eyes peering out from the branches. It made me laugh.

Inside, the card read, "Remember to sleep in stardust. I'll be waving through heaven's window. Love, your friend Dinky. P.S. I'll hug your daddy for you."

Even now, ever so many years later, some nights moonlight streams in the windows of my little house and fills it with stardust. I move my pillow until it's covered and then fall asleep smiling.

THE KALEIDOSCOPE

Friday afternoon
Main Street, Brighton, Michigan
Stephanie Flynn stood outside the stained-glass store in her small hometown and fumed. "Why should I have to do this? I'm not an artist, and all I would do is embarrass myself." Finally, after weighing her options, she turned and walked away.

Monday morning
Psychologist Dr. Amanda Atkins's office
"Hi, Stephanie," the slender, dark-haired doctor chimed in her upbeat way.

"Hello, Dr. Atkins." Stephanie wished she had worked up the courage to skip this appointment. But she already had demonstrated her lack of courage when she had stood in front of that store last Friday.

"Well, how was your first glass class?" Dr. Atkins smiled, as she tossed her long hair over her shoulder.

"I didn't go." Stephanie could feel her stomach muscles tensing.

"Really? Do you want to talk about it?" Dr. Atkins leaned in toward Stephanie.

"Not particularly." Stephanie crossed her arms. She felt uncomfortable with the silence that followed, but she refused to elaborate.

Finally Dr. Atkins asked, "Stephanie, why did we decide attending a stained-glass class would be good for you?"

"You said that I needed to be involved in my own healing journey and that you thought this class would help. But I'm paying you to fix me, to patch me up; so why should I have to traipse off to some glue-gun class to make a stupid lampshade? It doesn't make any sense," she added.

"We've been over this before, Stephanie. I can't fix you. I can listen, suggest, guide, but I don't have the power to fix someone else."

"I know, I know."

"We're each responsible for our own progress, and progress comes through teachability, truth, time, and risk. It *is* a risk to try something outside our scope of experience."

"I have to say that taking a class feels like I'd be in way over my head." Stephanie's voice was flat.

"What's the worst thing that ever happened to you when you took a risk?"

Stephanie thought for a while. Then her throat constricted, and she looked down at her hands to avoid Dr. Atkins's gaze. The hands were strangling each other.

"You thought of something, didn't you?" Dr. Atkins prompted.

"Yes. But, but it was a risk I never took." Stephanie still stared at her hands, clutched together.

"Tell me about it." The words were soft as a down comforter.

"When I was about seven," Stephanie began, "our family stayed at some friends' cottage overnight. They lived on a lake, and everyone in our group could swim but me. Even my younger sister was like a tadpole. I sat on the dock and dangled my feet in the water until my dad insisted I jump in where it was over my head. I pleaded with him not to make me, but he just got madder. He dragged me behind a shed where he lit into me with his belt for making him look bad in front of the others. The welts were so deep on my skinny little legs that I couldn't wear a bathing suit the rest of the summer." Stephanie shuddered, remembering the pain.

"What your dad did was cruel," Dr. Atkins said. "What he asked of you was threatening, and your response was natural and appropriate. If this stained-glass class feels too much like that, too risky for you, by all means let's wait until you feel it's time."

Another silent pause lay between the two women. Finally Stephanie said, "No, I guess I know it's time, but when I'm faced with something I'm uncertain I can do, I feel like that helpless child on the end of the dock. Even simple challenges overwhelm me."

"Is that what you felt when you thought about signing up for the class? Intimidated?"

"Actually, I felt anger. In fact, I was ticked at you for putting me in that…that…intimidating position."

"Anger seems to be your response when you don't feel safe, doesn't it?"

"I felt resentment that you had asked me to do something I didn't know how to do." Anger flicked alive inside Stephanie's chest, as if, by Dr. Atkins's giving the emotion a name, it had burst into flame.

"Who would you say attends a beginner's class, Stephanie?" the doctor inquired.

"Beginners, of course. But I would bet they're all artistic."

"Didn't you tell me once you made that jacket you're wearing?"

"Well, yes, but sewing isn't hard."

"Stephanie, you are artistic. In fact, we're all artistic. Some folks do portraits in charcoal while others paint pictures with words. Some knit sweaters, and their friends cook meals that delight the eye as well as the taste buds. If your sewing comes naturally for you, it doesn't mean what you produce isn't artistic; instead, it suggests your seamstress work is a gift. A gift flows from your life with minimal effort. The rest of life, though, tends to be work, not easy, but worth the moxie it takes to stretch beyond what comes easily."

"Okay, okay. I'll try," Stephanie conceded.

"You need to do this for yourself, not for me."

"I want to be able to dive in the deep end of the pool and swim."

"Stephanie, you're making wonderful progress. I'm proud of the way you're working through hard conversations."

"What, like this one?" A smile edged onto Stephanie's face.

"Exactly," the doctor responded warmly.

Wednesday

Inside the Kaleidoscope Stained-Glass Store

"I'd like to sign up for a class," Stephanie requested of the tall, blond man behind the counter. She noted his gentle hands as he placed a delicate figurine in the showcase. The suede vest he wore over his moss green turtleneck gave his thirtyish appearance an appealing warmth.

"Are you a beginner or an intermediate?" he asked with a smile.

"Actually, I'd fit best in a preschooler group because I know nothing about stained glass." Stephanie's voice was edged in reluctance.

"Trust me, you won't be alone. Several of the students will be newcomers to glasswork. I'll help you every step of the way to make sure your experience is as positive as possible. I want you to enjoy yourself. If you don't, you won't come back, and that would be bad for business."

They both chuckled.

Maybe, just maybe, this won't be so awful after all.

"Here's a list of the items you'll need for the class. My name is Bryan. Why don't you look around the store to familiarize yourself with the surroundings? Our work area is in the back, our glass is in the slots lining both walls, and the tools you'll need are in the two showcases. You might want to use our tools for your first project until you see if you'd like to buy your own. That's up to you. If you need help finding anything, just let me know."

"Thanks, Bryan." Stephanie turned and headed toward the glass, wondering if Bryan was watching her. She didn't dare turn around to find out. Instead, she studied the glass and noted it came in different size sheets and in a myriad of colors. Some of the glass was translucent while other sheets were solid colors. There were sheets of glass with swirls; some had wisps like clouds floating through them; others had an iridescent quality to them.

Stephanie was most drawn to the aqua and purple translucent sheets, especially when she held them up to the light. She couldn't imagine cutting this beautiful glass.

According to the itemized list, the project would be a multicolored heart that would hang in a window to catch the light. The heart was to be composed of ten small pieces of glass surrounded by four larger pieces of clear, beveled glass. Stephanie settled on purple, aqua, yellow, and blue glass for her heart. By the time she found everything on her list, her enthusiasm for the class was building.

After paying for her supplies, Stephanie was headed for the front door when she saw an arrangement of kaleidoscopes on a table in the gift section. Unable to resist a peek, she set down her packages, picked up one of the kaleidoscopes, and held it to her eye. Colored flecks of glass danced in crazy patterns as she rocked the scope back and forth. Each formation used shape and color to make dazzling arrangements. Stephanie, at thirty-two, felt like a kid again, which for her was a mixed blessing.

She was about to turn and leave when she spotted the granddaddy of all kaleidoscopes near the front showcase window. Amazed at its size, Stephanie hurried over to take a closer look. The huge kaleidoscope was nested on a tripod, and the giant lens was directed toward the natural light pouring in through the window. She leaned down and gasped at the beauty before her eyes. Large chunks of broken glass cartwheeled in cascades of color—oranges, reds, blues, yellows, greens, purples, blacks, and whites. Within moments she was lost in the tumbling world of color and light.

"Fun, isn't it?" Bryan asked as he straightened glassware on a nearby shelf.

"Oh, Bryan, it's wonderful. It must be pricey."

"It's for display only. My uncle designed it and gave it to me at the opening of the store."

"What a captivating gift." Stephanie found she had a growing fascination with the kaleidoscopes, not to mention their owner.

"Yeah, there's just something about contained color and light that's almost magical."

Tearing herself away, Stephanie gathered her packages and assured Bryan she would return for class the following week.

Later that evening
Stephanie Flynn's home, 626 Oak Leaf Lane

Stephanie held the refrigerator door open with her foot and unloaded her armful of groceries: yogurt, orange juice, pears, and cheese. She realized the fridge needed to be cleaned out as she removed a bowl of furry beets and headed for the garbage can. As a single gal she seemed always to have more food than she could eat.

While Stephanie busied herself about the kitchen, she thought of her week. She chuckled at her reluctance to sign up for the stained-glass class, realizing that, once again, she had made too big a deal out of something simple. "When will I learn not to make life more difficult than it is? And when will I nip in the bud my tendency to look at life's opportunities through negative lenses?" But then, it was a Flynn attribute to be pessimistic as surely as it was to have a wide jaw and cavernous dimples.

Stephanie's mind wandered back to Iowa and the Flynn farm where she was raised and where the silken cornfields stood in rows as far as the eye could see. As a child, she would dream of those stalks turning into soldiers and then marching away in the night, leaving the landscape barren. That was actually a wish more than a dream because she knew the closer harvest time came the meaner her father would become. The added stress of bringing in the crops, the poor prices they would fetch, and the impending winter seemed to set off her father. His tirades were as cyclical as the crops and as cutting as a scythe.

Stephanie and her sister, Suzanne, were prompted by their mom weeks in advance to stay out of their dad's path as much as possible and to obey his requests without hesitation. Try as they might, something always went awry.

Stephanie remembered the time she and her sister were playing hide-and-seek outside. Deciding to trick her sister, Stephanie hid inside the house. When Suzanne covered her eyes and began to count, Stephanie slipped into the kitchen, locking the door behind her so that Suzanne would have to go around to the front of the house to get in. After a moment

Stephanie decided to hide in the broom closet in the pantry.

Within a couple of minutes, she heard the doorknob being jiggled, and she began to giggle. But then she heard her father bellow, "Who locked this door?"

At first Stephanie was paralyzed with fear. Then she realized she was the only one in the house, and she would have to open the door. By the time she stepped out of the closet and into the kitchen, she saw two unforgettable sights. One was her father's outraged face, and the other was his fist moving through the air and then through the window. The shattered glass flew across the kitchen in all directions.

Stephanie, frozen at the pantry door, watched as her father, with his bloodied fist, unlocked the door and stepped into the kitchen. Within a moment he had her by her shoulders, shaking her until she feared she would black out. Cursing, he set her down hard and told her to clean up the mess. Dizzy and nauseated, she stumbled about, trying to pick up the shards and slivers of glass that had showered onto the floor...

The telephone's ring jolted Stephanie out of her childhood memory.

"Hello, I'm calling from the Worldwide Survey Alliance," Stephanie heard a male voice say when she lifted the receiver. "I was wondering if you could answer a few questions for us regarding your use of certain products in your home."

"No, I will not! And why don't you get yourself a real job and quit annoying people?" Stephanie slammed down the receiver. But as she walked away from the phone, another voice came to her, Dr. Atkins's. *Anger seems to be your response when you don't feel safe.*

Then Stephanie realized that, as she had relived the kitchen experience and her dad's explosive temper, she had broken into a sweat. She noted the tightness in her stomach and the level of her frustration. The young man's pleasant voice passed through Stephanie's mind again, and she felt sad about her harsh reaction. It made her wonder how many other people had been victims of her misguided anger.

Later that night, she settled into her bed to write about her feelings. She had been journaling for four months, an exercise she began at Dr. Atkins's recommendation. At first Stephanie found the writing tedious and disruptive both to her schedule and her emotions, but now it had become a part of her routine and often was cathartic to her soul. The journaling seemed to give her a place not only to fully form her feelings, but also, after she had made an entry, to have more space inside herself, as though she had made room for other feelings.

Tonight her anger was what she wanted to write about.

Dear Phone Man,

If I knew your name, I would write you an apology, but since I don't, placing you in my journal is the best I can do. I'm sorry I snapped at you. I'm sure your sales profession isn't easy, and I had no right to suggest your work wasn't a real job. I can only imagine how difficult your job is.

If I could sit across the table from you, I would tell you that your call jarred me out of an unpleasant memory that had me tied in knots. I was remembering my explosive father, and then what did I do but turn around and act just like him. God forbid. You see, my dad was a rageaholic. Everything made him angry.

I recall one time, after I had gathered eggs from the hen-house, I didn't latch the gate well on the way out. My dad came around the corner just then, spotted the open gate, and went berserk. He snatched the basket from my hand and smashed every egg with his size eleven work boots. It scared me so bad I wet my pants. When I made it to the safety of my room, feeling both afraid and humiliated, instead of crying, I ripped my pillow apart. Perhaps it was then I began to make anger my refuge instead of feeling my fear and allowing it to run its course. And maybe the intensity and intimidation of my dad's behavior was more than a child could bear.

Dr. Atkins told me that anger makes us feel more in control of our circumstances, even when we're not. And in my family, our ranting dad was the one in charge. I wonder what he was afraid of?

Anyway, telephone man, forgive me for spewing my fear and anger all over you.

That Wednesday, as Stephanie ventured out to attend her first class, she found herself, instead, stuck in traffic, which overflowed from the nearby large city into her small community at the end of the day. She could see she was going to be late, and tardiness went against her grain. As the minutes ticked away, she began to consider a way out of this snarl of cars. She pulled onto the road's shoulder, passed two cars, made a right into Stop & Shop, and then drove through Carney's gas station, making a right onto Second Street. On her way at last!

When she turned into the parking lot behind The Kaleidoscope, she heard a siren. Her neck tensed as she saw in her rearview mirror that a police car had followed her, lights ablaze, into the lot. She pulled into a parking spot and rolled down her window as she reached for her purse. That was when she noticed several people from The Kaleidoscope looking out the window to see what was going on.

"Oh, great," she moaned, wishing the officer would turn off his twirling lights.

"I'd like to see your driver's license, miss," he stated as he approached her window.

"Shouldn't you be out catching bank robbers?" Stephanie retorted in a low voice.

"Yes, bank robbers and individuals who put other people's lives in jeopardy by careless driving maneuvers."

"Touché. Of course you're right." She sat quietly while he wrote her up.

After the officer presented Stephanie with a hefty ticket, she was up against another unpleasant task: facing her new classmates. They knew she had broken the law, and she was embarrassed. She sat for several minutes trying to sort through her jumbled feelings and was considering leaving when she heard a tap on her window. Looking up, she saw Bryan smiling down at her. She expected some sarcastic remark about her driving, but instead Bryan asked, "May I help you carry your supplies? The class has begun, but it will only take a few minutes for me to help you get started."

Relieved at his kindness, Stephanie accepted his offer and followed him in. As she trailed him down the hall to the work area, she chuckled to herself. *This reminds me of the lost lamb story where the Good Shepherd goes out to rescue the wayward lamb.* She wondered how Bryan felt shepherding a renegade sheep.

When they entered the workroom, several class members glanced up and nodded. Stephanie couldn't tell if their smiles were friendly or if they were amused at her brush with the law. Bryan ushered her over to a stool and placed her bag of supplies on the expansive worktable.

On one side of Stephanie was a red-headed woman wearing thick glasses who hovered over her project. On the other side was a balding, fortyish-looking man, Dennis, who looked at her and quipped, "Hi ya, Hot Rod." Snickers spread around the table like a brush fire, and the smiling Dennis seemed pleased.

Stephanie's face flushed, but she knew she deserved to be teased. Besides, the laughter broke the tension, and now they could all get on with the class. Bryan instructed her on how to cut out her pattern pieces and place them on her glass. Next she was to cut around the pattern with glass cutters and then smooth each piece with a grinder and grouser.

Once Stephanie had her pattern cut out and in place, she picked up her glass cutters and began to snip. She was feeling unsure of what she was doing, and her hands perspired.

At one point she pressed wrong, and the sheet of glass slipped from her hand and shattered on the floor. Suddenly she was in the farm's kitchen again, with her father smashing the door's window. Old fear tightened in her stomach.

"Don't worry. It happens to everyone. I'll be right back with a new sheet." Bryan smiled at her and left to retrieve the glass.

Stephanie let out the air she had been holding in her lungs, as if the memory had thrust her underwater where it wasn't safe to breathe. She smiled back at Bryan when he returned.

Dennis found a broom and swept up the mess while Bryan helped Stephanie to replace her pattern. Then Bryan extracted a pair of cutters from his work apron and began to snip. She appreciated his nonchalant response, which made her feel less like a klutz. Obviously he was keeping his promise to help her succeed. By the time the class was over, she had almost caught up to the others.

Stephanie thanked Bryan for his help and kindness. She wasn't sure, but she almost thought he blushed. On her way home she wondered exactly how old Bryan was. He had one of those ageless faces. She guessed him to be somewhere around her age, maybe a few years older. His easy smile added to his soft countenance, which Stephanie found appealing. Of course, she reminded herself, for all she knew he might be married with six kids.

The next morning, Stephanie was sitting at the breakfast table finishing her last cup of coffee when the phone rang.

"Hello, Stephanie?" a male voice inquired.

"Yes, this is Stephanie."

"This is Bryan from The Kaleidoscope. I hope I didn't wake you."

Stephanie felt her heart flutter. "No, not at all. In fact, I'm almost ready to head off to work."

"I won't keep you. I just wanted to offer you some help with your project. You probably could catch up with the rest of the class if you put in half an hour."

"Thanks, Bryan. I appreciate your call. Yesterday didn't go quite the way I had planned. Next time I'll leave for class a little earlier so I won't be tempted to pull any rodeo stunts with my car and drag a posse in tow with me." Stephanie heard him gently laugh, and she noticed that pleased her. "I get off work at six this evening. Would that be too late to stop in?"

"That would work fine for me."

"Great, see you then." Stephanie hung up the phone and discovered she had a fresh interest in the day. In fact, she found herself humming right through work to quitting time.

That evening Stephanie considered going to a restaurant drive-through to pick up a quick bite to eat but decided against it. She didn't want to be late again. When she entered the store, Bryan was with a customer so she headed for the big kaleidoscope in the window. She gave it a twirl, but the colors had no brilliance or sparkle. Realizing that the sun was too far down to give the needed light, she turned the scope toward the ceiling light and twirled again. This time the colors were lively, and they tumbled about in topsy-turvy patterns that delighted her.

"I'm glad you like Miss Caprice," Bryan said.

"Miss Caprice?" Stephanie looked up into Bryan's smiling face, and her heart skipped a beat.

"A nickname I gave the kaleidoscope for her whimsical, ever-changing ways. In fact, I'd like to show you something." Bryan stepped over to a display case, opened a drawer, and took something out. "Open your hands."

She did, and he filled them with colored glass in different sizes and shapes. "This is what's inside Miss Caprice."

"Oh, they look so ordinary, so drab."

"It's when the colors are held up to the light that all the dynamics occur."

"Looking at these glass shards now, with no light to show them off, I would never guess they could be so beautiful."

"Yeah, it's sort of the same with our lives, when you think about it. No matter how damaged we are, when we hold up the broken pieces to the light of truth, we see our own potential for beauty."

Stephanie stared at him for a moment and then grinned suspiciously. "Did my counselor tell you to say that?"

Bryan laughed. "No, actually my therapist helped me to see that."

Stephanie found herself liking this man more and more. Yet she still didn't know for sure if he was available or if he was interested in her. She thought it romantic that they were working on her heart project together.

As they settled into working on the heart, Stephanie found she enjoyed holding the colored glass and watching the light illuminate it, but she was still tentative when it was time to cut it. She was afraid she would shatter her own efforts.

Once the pieces were cut, she liked softening the edges and placing the pieces into her pattern. And Bryan let her practice her soldering on some throwaway glass before the next class, when she would need to do it for real. Her solder lines were a little wiggly, but she could tell she was improving.

When they finished for the evening, Bryan surprised her by bringing out a tray filled with finger sandwiches and cheesecake. "I wondered if you'd like to join me for a quick dinner," he asked casually. "I figured since you were coming here from work you might not have had a chance to grab anything. I usually eat and then take a walk around the mill pond before calling it a night."

"I'm starved. Thanks, Bryan. Did you make this up yourself?"

"Oh no, I cheated. I used the deli across the street; their cheesecake is the best. I'm a terrible cook, but I excel at takeout."

The evening was even more delicious than the cheesecake as far as Stephanie was concerned. After they ate, she joined Bryan for his walk. She found him easy to be around.

By the time Stephanie arrived home, she knew she had a crush on this sensitive man. She went right to her journal and began a new entry.

Dear Bryan,

So help me if I find out you're married, I'll scream. I'll forget all I've been learning about my fear and anger issues, and I'll throw a major hissy fit. You are so dear and kind and thoughtful. The men I've been close to have been angry, insensitive louts. Uh-oh, some of my anger is seeping out again. But, Bryan, they haven't been the kind of men who realized they were fractured much less men who would work on their issues like you. You have the sweetest smile and the dearest laugh.

I'm sounding like a schoolgirl or a desperate single woman. Oh my, where is Dr. Atkins when I need her?

Monday evening
Dr. Atkins's office

"My advice, since you asked for it," Dr. Atkins said after Stephanie had recounted her budding interest in Bryan, "would be to slow down. You're working on some important issues that affect your personal relationships. Jumping into a romance can complicate things. Besides, you don't know that's his intent."

Stephanie didn't say anything, but the way she squirmed in her chair and wouldn't look at Dr. Atkins probably communicated plenty about how she felt.

Dr. Atkins studied her for a moment and then said, "You're more vulnerable when you're dealing with old wounds, and it would be easy to want a gentle man, someone unlike your daddy, to soothe your hurting heart. What you need long-term is not soothing but healing and closure. That's not to say that gentle people in your life wouldn't help; we all respond to kindness. Just don't expect others to erase your interior pain for you."

"That's not the answer I wanted," Stephanie finally remarked curtly.

"I don't blame you, Stephanie. I wish there were easier answers."

By the time Wednesday arrived, Stephanie thought she just wouldn't show up for class, but she decided running from her problems wouldn't help.

Then she wondered if she was fooling herself so she could see Bryan again. This was getting complicated, just like Dr. Atkins had said.

Drat Dr. Atkins. She got me in this mess. Deep down Stephanie knew that wasn't true; she couldn't hold Dr. Atkins responsible for Stephanie's erratic heart. So Stephanie decided she would attend class.

The time flew by as they learned how to foil, flux, and solder their pieces. Bryan circled the room, answering questions and assisting when necessary. When Bryan was busy with someone else's project, the ever-quipping Dennis would help keep Stephanie on track. He was a jovial soul who easily made everyone laugh with his mischievous ways, and yet he learned fast and was quick to help others. Because of Bryan and Dennis's joint effort, by the end of the evening each class member held with pride a completed project.

Stephanie lifted up her multicolored heart to watch as the light danced through it.

"Hey, Hot Rod, your heart looks like a patchwork quilt," Dennis said.

"You're right about that," Stephanie replied, wishing Dennis wasn't always so verbal—or so accurate.

Then Bryan announced a second class for those who would like to continue and passed around a sign-up sheet. Stephanie packed up her tools and was headed for the door when Bryan called to her. As he approached, he said, "I was disappointed your name wasn't on the sign-up list. Didn't you enjoy yourself?"

"Yes, I did. It's just that my counseling requires my undivided attention right now. But I'd love to come back in a few months and try again." The gentle fragrance of his aftershave caused Stephanie's resolve to weaken.

"It's a deal. If I can ever be a listening ear for you or a friend to eat sandwiches with, just give me a jingle. Or if you'd like to visit Miss Caprice, stop by and give her a spin."

"You've been so nice to me. Thank you." Stephanie could feel herself choking up.

"Being nice to you wasn't hard at all," Bryan half whispered, and she could tell he meant it.

Two nights later, Stephanie set aside time to pen her thoughts.

Dear Journal,

I had the strangest dream last night. I found myself in a long room. The walls were lined with glass, but the building had no roof, which allowed the light to be reflected off the myriad pieces of colored glass. Transparent rainbows seemed to fill the room with a warm glow. An angelic being entered, but instead of using the perfect sheets of glass, he took a broom and swept up shards from under the workstation, in the corners, and from behind the counter. He scooped the fragments into a basket and poured them out onto the table. Then he pulled out some sterling tools from a golden box and leaned over the smudged glass. Some of the shards had rough edges, and some were actually jagged. Many were oddly shaped, and all of them were coated in dust. These were throwaway pieces, ones that had been unsalvageable, ones that had been dropped, walked on, and forgotten.

I don't know how long the angel hovered over his work, but he pursued his objective intently. He softened the jagged corners, reshaped the distorted ones, and polished each broken piece. Then he brought out a form from underneath the table and fit the pieces into it.

I moved closer to see this glass puzzle and was amazed that it took every piece to finish the pattern. I watched as he soldered, each silver seam drawing the pieces together into a design. When he removed the form, he hung the creation on a hook in the center of the room, and then he knelt as though he was praying.

I looked up, and my breath caught in my throat. From all the brokenness he had designed a cross...a dazzling, patchwork cross.

I awoke unsure of all the dream's meaning but certain my wholeness was part of God's ultimate plan.

One year and five months later
Stephanie's home

Dear Lord,

Whew, what a journey! I've never worked harder nor have I ever felt better. I've had my ups, and I certainly have had my downs. It's been so good to find that wherever I am on my emotional chart, You, Lord, have always been there with me and for me. I've been ever changing. And You, Lord, have been immutable.

I could never have guessed the path You had in mind for me. Thank You for not only bringing healing to my heart, but for the one You have given me to love. Thank You that he is a gentle man who acknowledges You and is able to face even the worst of his own heart, knowing You love him. I love him, too, Lord. Deeply. Thank You.

Stephanie

Later that evening, Stephanie wrote this note:

Dear Bryan,

I'm left breathless by your gift. You sure know how to make a wedding special. When Miss Caprice arrived at my door, I was euphoric. What an extravagant thing to do! Thank you beyond what words can express.

Love, Stephanie & Dennis

P.S. Dennis likes "her" almost as much as I do.

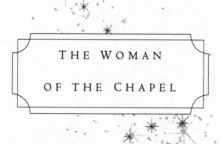

THE WOMAN
OF THE CHAPEL

*T*he old man stood slowly, his body creaking like an ancient door. The roadside boulder where he had sat resting marked the beginning of his day. He rubbed his eyes, trying to force the sunlight from blinding his already poor vision, and then shaded his face with his hands as he began his rounds. He would stop first at Emanuel's to fill the fellow's bucket with water from the pump in the yard. Emanuel had fallen in the mines and would be laid up for some time, so the old man had volunteered to check in on him.

When the old man entered Emanuel's home, he found Emanuel, his dark hair spilling onto the pillow, asleep and ever so still.

"Hello," the old man whispered.

Emanuel didn't respond.

"Hello," the old fellow said more emphatically.

Emanuel's eyes fluttered. "Hello, my friend."

"Is it well with you?" the old man asked as he stepped closer to the bedside.

"As well as can be," Emanuel said in a voice filled with both sadness and promise.

"How might I ease your pain?" the old man inquired.

"Sit and tell me of yourself," the invalid said.

The old man filled the pail and set it back near Emanuel's bedside, placing the dipper at his patient's fingertips. Then, with some effort, the old man pulled a wooden chair next to the bedside and sat down.

"What shall I tell you today?"

"Tell me of her, the Woman of the Chapel."

"But we talked of her yesterday."

"Yes, yes, I know. Tell me again."

The old man put his face in his hands for several moments to steady his thoughts and then, lifting his head, he began. "She was lovely. Her raven hair caught the sun as she worked in the fields. Her eyes were full of tender mercies, and her hands were gentle and strong. She was a wisp of a woman with mightiness at her core; her spirit drew the people to her. Each evening, after the fields, she would go to the chapel where workers would ask her to pray for them and their families. They would bring their children, and she would enfold them in her arms and whisper up prayers like sweet incense. Sick children would be strengthened, frantic babies would become still in her arms, and families would be drawn together in her presence." The old man reached in his pocket and pulled out a tattered handkerchief to mop his moist brow. "Enough of her today. I must continue my journey."

"So soon, old friend?"

"Tomorrow I will return. Your sister will be home by sunset to fix you supper, won't she?"

"Yes."

The old man rose, steadying himself against the bed until he gained his footing. Then he walked over to the kitchen table and picked up an apple from the fruit bowl. With his bent fingers he polished it with a cloth and placed the fruit in Emanuel's hand. "Rest well, heal quickly. God be with you," the old man uttered, and then he left.

An hour later, with some effort, the old man bent down to enter a small cottage. "Anna, it is me, your friend. I have brought you medicine for the child."

A young mother, with her arms full of child, approached him. "Let me see," she asked, as if she feared it could not be true.

He removed a small vial from his pocket and carefully handed her the liquid. Her eyes welled with tears.

The old man eased himself down into a nearby rocker and put out his arms for the child. The mother transferred the frail, whimpering one into his arms.

"You rest. I will rock," he instructed.

The mother lay down on a daybed in the corner and within moments was sound asleep. The old man rocked the child and sang softly of heaven. Two hours passed before the mother stirred.

"I've slept much too long. I'm sorry," she said as she rushed to relieve the old man of his duty. When the child was in her arms again, she sat at the old man's feet and asked, "Will you speak of her today?"

"For a moment." He paused, his arms aching where the child had lain in them. Then he said, "Her voice was like a brook singing of its Maker. People listened carefully to what she said, for the wisdom of the ages rested on her tongue. She spoke of heaven and hardships in one breath, knowing one would help us overcome the other. Wherever she went, birds sang and children laughed."

The old man leaned forward, placing his gnarled hand on the young woman's head. "May peace reign in your mind and Christ rule your heart."

"God go with you, old man."

"And with you, child."

The sun was resting on the treetops, turning them crimson, as the old man headed toward the outskirts of town. He hummed even though he could only shamble along. Stopping at a set of rickety gates, he caught his labored breath and opened the gates. Soon several cows sauntered through the opening and down the dirt road. The old man trailed behind them until he safely steered them into a shabby lean-to. He tapped on the door of the nearby home, and an elderly woman opened the door and motioned him in.

"I cannot visit. I must go now. Your cows are home," he told her.

"Old man, sit and have bread with me and then be on your way."

Feeling his need for nourishment, he heeded her invitation and sat down to dine on hard bread, cheese, and cool drafts of cow's milk. When he finished, the woman asked, "Will you leave me with a word of her before you depart?"

"Yes, yes, of course," he answered. "The Woman of the Chapel walked in heaven's graces. A covering of kindness rested on her like a mantle that she extended to those she met. She mended lives with forgiveness and sowed seeds of the Savior's love. Her strength was in her meekness."

His hostess listened carefully to each word about the woman whose life had become a legend in their village. The old man was the only one left who had known her. Some said he had loved her and she him, but the old man never spoke of their feelings for each other, and no one dared to ask lest he be offended. The townspeople did not know her name, and the old man never said. For most, because of her devotion to prayer, she was known simply as the Woman of the Chapel.

After the old man left, he trudged through the darkness until he came to a narrow path that led to a barn. The smell of animals and hay filled his nostrils and brought him relief, for this was home. He could rest soon. He greeted the goats by name as he filled their troughs and patted their heads. He offered hay to the horses and feed to the chickens and then sat down on a stool next to a cow, soothing her with his words. Soon he had drawn from her fullness a half-pail of milk. He thanked her and carried the pail to the house. The old man tapped on the door.

"Come in, old man. You are once again home safely. I thank God for your return." The greeting was from the owner of the home, a crippled man, Jesse. He sat twisted in a chair, smiling at the sight of his friend. "Do you have strength to tell me of your journey?"

The old man pulled a cup off a hook on the wall, poured Jesse some milk, and placed it by his chair. "The road was long, the people good, and God gracious."

"And did they ask of the woman?"

"Yes, everywhere they ask of her. She is a legend."

"Ah, but only because of your devoted offerings. You have kept her faith alive with your stories," Jesse replied softly.

"As it should be. Her deep well of kindness should be ladled up to the lips of the thirsty. She brought Christ's hope to those crushed by life's hardness."

"You loved her, didn't you?" Jesse looked hesitant, as though his probing question might have crossed the line with the old man.

"Many loved her. She mirrored the Savior. One could not help but be drawn to His beauty in her."

"When did you first meet her?"

"In the wheat fields. I found her kneeling with a small wounded bird cupped in her hands. Her tears fell onto the bird, and suddenly he stretched his wings and flew. She looked up toward heaven and whispered, 'Thank you.'"

"How did she die?"

The old man sat in silence. Minutes ticked by until finally he spoke. "We do not know. I found her in the chapel. She appeared to be asleep, and, in fact, she was. Asleep in Christ. Above her, in the rafters, was a small bird singing passionately. Even after her body was removed the bird continued to sing praises. It sounded like an aria, a divine aria."

The old man stood; he smiled at his crippled friend and quietly sang, "God keep you in the night, wake you with a song, may you know His delight, to Him you belong."

Jesse nodded his head and added, "Amen."

"May I help you to the bed before I leave?"

"Yes, please."

The old man leaned down, and with strength beyond his own, he carefully shouldered Jesse's weight and guided him to bed. Hesitating a moment, the old man looked down at Jesse's broken body and said, "It will not always be this way for you, my friend. One day, Jesse, you will leap for joy."

Jesse's eyes filled, and with emotion he choked out, "God go with you."

"And with you," the old man called back, as he shuffled through the door.

The moonlight led the ancient man back to the barn where he opened a stall and sank down onto his blanket spread out on the hay. That night his dreams were full of gossamer wings and heavenly sounds.

The following afternoon Jesse's neighbor found the old man asleep in the hay. The strain of his life had left his face, and blessed relief covered his countenance. Overhead the sweet song of a small bird filled the air.

Word spread throughout the village of the old man's departure, and soon the villagers came to hear the song of heaven from the tiny, winged messenger. The old man's body was buried across from the Woman of the Chapel's grave site.

Months passed, and winter moved into the village. A male figure with a decided limp made his way to the door of a cottage and tapped on the window. A feeble woman opened the door, and the man hobbled in. Slowly he limped to her fireplace and added his bundle of sticks. Soon the fire blazed.

"Is it well with you?" he asked of her.

"It is better now. Do you bring me word of him?"

"Yes, yes I do," Emanuel answered. "I cannot stay long for the road ahead is full, but for this moment we will talk." And then he began. "The Old Man moved through our village with strength born from pain. He quietly brought cheer to the downtrodden, goodwill his constant companion. The Old Man's eyes held eternity's shore, and his heart's cup poured forth tenderness on earth's rocky existence. He walked bent from his servanthood yet stood upright before the Lord. I never knew his name. He was known simply as 'the Old Man.'"

The two huddled close to the fire and each other, warming themselves with stories that added heaven's heart to humanity...and they were comforted.

RUNAWAY

Banty McCluster drew her satchel closer and stepped into line to insure that she would get a window seat near the front of the bus. Wisps of her nutmeg hair, heavily flecked with gray, slipped out from under her hat, which she had worn to protect her head from drafts. Banty hadn't traveled alone for many years, and she hoped no one would sit next to her. You never knew what kind of riffraff you might bump into these days. She had heard plenty of stories on the local newscasts about hooligans harassing senior citizens, and she didn't plan on being one of the victims. She just wanted to go home.

Home. What a wonderful sound to her ears. She had been away almost three years, three long, lonely years. On a bleak February day her son, Mark, had driven down to Boonville, Indiana, to move her up north to Milwaukee to live with his family. After Wendell, her husband of forty-seven years, had died that January, she had felt unsure of her own mind—except that she wasn't ready to sell the house. So when Mark insisted she move in with his family, she had.

Almost from the first day she had seen the arrangement was going to be awkward. Her daughter-in-law, Tricia, tried to tolerate an extra person in her space, but Banty kept bumping into her in one way or another. The children were a constant source of irritation, for even though they were Banty's own grandchildren and she loved them, they were ill-mannered rascals always into neighborhood scrapes. Why, just last week the two scamps were both sporting black eyes from their latest skirmishes.

But the most antagonistic family member was Mark, Banty's only son. She couldn't imagine what she and Wendell had done to produce such a quarrelsome individual. Mark was exhausting with his verbally combative attitude, taking on everyone from the weather reporter to the mail carrier, right down to the paper deliverer. Mark seemed to believe the world was out to make him miserable. And, from Banty's perspective, it had been successful. She decided parents should live in their own homes as long as possible, if for no other reason than to pretend their children had turned out better than they had.

"Here you go, ma'am. Watch your footing," the bus driver cautioned as he guided Banty by the elbow onto the bus steps.

Banty's diminutive stature afforded her many offers of assistance, most of which she had refused throughout her sixty-seven years, but today it just seemed easier to give in. She always had been spry and independent. Her granddaddy had named her Banty because she was such a lively newborn, reminding him of a feisty Banty rooster he once raised. Since Banty's mama already had seven children, she hadn't minded Granddaddy's input on the name. In fact, she was relieved to have help of any kind.

Banty found a window seat near the front and settled in, stuffing the satchel into the seat with her. She wasn't about to let it out of her sight; it held medicine, checkbook, wallet, house keys, Bible, lap quilt, and a manila envelope that was carefully wrapped in her sweater.

Tucking her hair back under her hat, Banty watched as others boarded. One bent-over, gray-haired man reeked of perspiration as he passed, making Banty feel queasy. A man with a three-inch facial scar and a leather jacket swaggered down the aisle as if he was looking for trouble. And an elderly couple in tattered clothes seemed like lost souls searching for a destination. They held on to each other as if they were equally afraid.

Banty found herself praying, "Lord, please don't let any unsavory person sit next to me. I need Your protection. Help me to get home safely. Amen."

Voices rose from outside the bus door, as did the sound of scuffling. Banty peeked out the window and saw the driver trying to discourage an inebriated man from boarding. The man became louder, more insistent, and combative. A tussle ensued, and a guard from the bus station was summoned. Soon the man was ushered away.

Banty's heart was pounding, and tears filled her eyes. She wondered if taking the bus had been a wise choice. Of course, she couldn't ask Mark to drive her because she hadn't told him she was going. She knew Mark would have fought her decision to return home, and she was tired of not being heard. She needed her own life back. Yes, she probably should have warned her son's family she was leaving, but she didn't want to slog through all the mire her decision would have created. So, instead, she had left a note they would find in the morning. By then Banty would be home.

"Excuse me," she heard a pleasant-looking woman say as she stepped past the portly driver and slipped into the row across from Banty.

Just seeing someone normal-looking was a relief to Banty. The woman appeared to be in her forties and was tastefully dressed in a yellow turtleneck sweater, tweed jacket, and black corduroy slacks. Her lovely, long blond hair was pulled back and held with a yellow ribbon. Banty wished the woman had sat next to her so they could enjoy the safety of each other's company. Within moments, though, a tall, lean, Levi's-clad man wearing cowboy boots sat down next to the woman, ending Banty's hopes of connecting with her.

A few minutes later Banty heard a baby's whimpers. When she looked up, a young woman with an infant on her shoulder stepped up from the stairwell into the bus. Banty decided the young gal must be part of a grunge group. Her dark hair was short and raucous with orange and green streaks. She sported a pierced eyebrow and nose, not to mention her pierced belly button that was exposed for public viewing. She was also displaying a butterfly tattoo on her midriff. All this was set off by skintight, black leather pants and platform shoes.

Banty found herself staring. Then, much to her consternation, the young woman plopped down in the seat next to her. Using her feet, the mother forced a diaper bag under the seat in front of her. Then she tried to reposition the baby in her arms so she could slip into the leather jacket she had tied around her hips. Banty couldn't help but note the long, black fingernails and wondered how the woman managed not to poke out her baby's eyes.

Then, without warning, she turned to Banty and said, "Here, hold Windsong while I get settled in. Thanks."

Why, she didn't even wait for me to agree. She just hoisted the baby into my arms. Banty was appalled at the mother's forwardness. The baby squirmed, and Banty looked into the blankets. The cherub-faced infant's pink cheeks and blue eyes caused Banty to smile in spite of her discontent with the child's brazen mama. Banty unconsciously patted the baby's arm.

The young mother once again gathered Windsong into her arms and cheerfully said, "Thanks. My name is Jade. Windsong is only six weeks old, but she's an armload already."

Banty nodded recognition that she heard Jade but didn't reply for fear Jade might take it as a gesture of friendship. Banty didn't believe in rushing into other people's lives unannounced. This Jade woman needed some etiquette lessons, not to mention a more appropriate wardrobe.

Now that Banty could see Jade up close she could tell she was just a girl wearing outlandish clothes and glittery makeup. Banty could only imagine what kind of wild lifestyle Jade was living.

The bus driver, after counting his passengers, took his seat, closed the door, and slowly pulled out of the depot. Banty, relieved they were finally moving, let out a sigh.

Jade leaned over and asked, "What's your name?"

Caught off guard, Banty cautiously replied, "Mrs. McCluster."

"Mrs. McCluster, don't you have a first name that folks call you?"

"Of course I do. Folks who have been properly introduced call me Banty. The rest call me Mrs. McCluster."

"Then I'll call you Banty, if that's okay with you." Jade smiled as she leaned down to pull a baby bottle out of the diaper bag's side pocket.

"If you need to call me, I'd prefer you use my proper name: Mrs. McCluster. Where I come from young people show regard for their elders." Banty tucked back another stray wisp of hair.

"And where I come from, folks at least try to be friendly," Jade retaliated. Then, nudging Windsong close, she began to feed the baby.

Banty couldn't decide whether she was insulted or convicted by Jade's remark. Banty had no desire to be Jade's friend, but she always had prided herself on her friendly nature. Or at least she was amiable with folks before Wendell died. In fact, he would tease Banty that she had never met a stranger. Perhaps the last few years, not getting out much, her people skills had lost their luster. Or maybe her grief and homesickness had caused her to act as miserable as she felt.

Banty decided not to think about all that now. She leaned back, closed her eyes, and listened to the tires' hum on the road and the gentle sounds of Windsong drinking her milk.

Banty dozed as the bus followed the ribboned highway south.

She was awakened by a frightening sound; the baby next to her was choking. Looking uncertain about what to do when patting Windsong briskly on the back failed, Jade began to shake her. Windsong's face had turned deep red from strangling, and her tiny body was stiff from the strain. Banty, seeing the baby's stress, pulled Windsong onto her lap and gently cleared her throat. Milk and phlegm, which had constricted her airway, spilled down the baby's front, but she began to breathe again. Banty handed the now wailing baby back to Jade to clean up and comfort.

Grabbing her satchel, Banty headed for the bathroom in the back to clean up as well, since her dress had been splattered with soured formula. When she returned, Windsong was lying quietly in her mother's arms, exhausted from her trauma.

Jade, looking unnerved, sat beside Banty for several miles before speaking. "Thank you, Mrs. McCluster. Thank you very much."

"You're welcome," Banty whispered.

Perhaps I've misjudged the girl. She does seem to be a devoted and attentive mother. But what kind of name is "Windsong" for a child? Well, I guess there's no law against strange names. If there were, "Banty" would probably head the list.

"Mrs. McCluster, let me pay to have your dress dry cleaned," Jade offered, reaching for her purse.

"No, my clothes are fine. It's nothing a little soap and water won't handle. Thank you for asking though." Banty smiled at Jade.

"Windsong is my first child. I guess I panicked. I'm the youngest in my family, so I'm not experienced, especially with emergencies."

"May I ask how old you are, Jade?" Banty knew she was being forward, but her curiosity had overtaken her good manners.

"I'm older than I look. I'm nineteen." Jade readjusted the baby's blankets.

"You're right. You look sixteen. That's a good problem to have," Banty said with a chuckle. "Are you on your way to visit family?"

"Yes, my oldest sister lives in Benson, Indiana. I'm going to stay with her for a while." Jade hesitated and then added, "I hope."

"Doesn't she know you're coming?"

"Well, no. You see, I'm running away." Jade dropped her eyes down toward Windsong.

"Running away from whom?"

"My husband." Tears began to drip onto the baby's nightgown. "We haven't been getting along. He wants me to work, but I don't want to leave my baby. So I just walked out." Jade looked up through her watery eyes at Banty.

"Running away from your problems doesn't solve them," Banty heard herself say.

"I know. But I just couldn't convince Jeff that Windsong needs me, and I didn't know what else to do."

"Did you leave him a note?"

"No. He wasn't going to be gone long, and I couldn't risk taking the extra time. I made the decision and acted on it in the same hour. That doesn't say much for my maturity, does it?"

Banty patted the young woman's arm. "Jade, we all make mistakes. I think not letting Jeff know that you and the baby are safe is a mistake. He must be very concerned right now."

The bus pulled into a diner, and the driver announced a thirty-minute stop. People began to file out to stretch, smoke, and grab coffee. Banty and Jade stayed on the bus and just sat quietly.

After ten minutes, Jade leaned over and touched Banty's arm. "Mrs. McCluster, would you hold Windsong for a few minutes while I run in to call Jeff?"

Banty nodded and opened her arms to receive the sleeping baby. While Jade was gone, Banty surveyed the tender new life as she rested. Windsong's rhythmic breathing, sporadically interrupted with a sigh and a little smile at the edge of her lips, reminded Banty of her own babies. Where had all the years gone? Now her babies were grown with babies of their own. Her mind focused on Mark, and she squirmed in her seat, realizing that, like a teenager, she, too, had run away instead of facing her family with her decision.

Soon a relieved Jade boarded the bus and took her seat. Reaching for Windsong, she said, "You were right, Mrs. McCluster. I'm glad I called. Jeff was really freaked. I said I'd call him later, when I arrived, and we could talk some more. I told him I was sorry I didn't leave a note. I couldn't tell if he was ticked or scared, but I just have a feeling we're going to be able to work this out after all."

"Jade, I think I'd better run in and make a phone call myself. Don't let the bus leave without me."

"I won't. I promise."

Banty returned a short time later with the bus driver once again at her elbow steadying her. Once on board, she stepped around Jade and Windsong and slipped into her seat. Banty knew she would travel easier now after speaking with Mark. Of course, she smiled to herself, she'd had the advantage when they talked since she had awakened him. Banty wasn't sure Mark's head ever really cleared as she confessed what she had done, but she knew by morning he would figure it all out. They could talk more then.

The bus driver announced that the next stop was two hours down the line. He once again counted his passengers, and then, wrapping his arms around the massive steering wheel, he pulled back onto the now deserted highway. Soon the night rhythms caused heads to become heavy with sleep. Banty, feeling chilled, pulled on her long, cozy sweater and tried to read her Bible, but she was concerned that the reading light's glare would disturb Windsong. So instead Banty tucked her book down inside her roomy sweater pocket and turned out the light.

Banty dozed, but every sound seemed to rouse her. At one point she was aware of movement across the aisle, and when she opened her eyes, Banty saw the attractive woman slip out of her seat and walk toward the driver. Wondering if the woman had a problem, Banty leaned forward and saw her say something to the driver that caused him to slow the bus and pull it off the road. It came to a stop in a deserted rest area. The braking caused other passengers to stir from their sleep.

"This is a holdup. I'm armed, and I'm not alone," a man shouted from the back of the bus. "Don't act foolish, and you won't get hurt."

Confused, Banty looked toward the bus driver again. That's when she saw the woman was brandishing a small handgun.

Banty's heart began to palpitate as she realized the danger they all were in. The lean man who had been seated next to this woman was in the back with a semiautomatic rifle, yelling for everyone to empty the contents of their purses and wallets into a box he was kicking down the aisle, row by row. "Don't anyone try to be a hero because I'll blow your head off," he threatened.

Banty's mind went to her satchel and the manila envelope that held her life savings. She slowly slipped her trembling hand into the satchel at her side and fished out the envelope. Then she tried to slip it under her dress.

Jade saw the desperation in Banty's eyes and reached for the envelope. Banty held it tightly until she realized she would have to trust Jade, who carefully slid it between the blankets wrapped around Windsong.

"What are you doing?" the woman screamed at Jade, pointing the gun in her direction.

"I'm trying to straighten my baby's blankets," she responded with a quaver in her voice.

"Well, stop moving around or that baby won't have a mother. Understand?" The woman's eyes flared with rage.

"Yes, I'll be still."

Banty reached in the dark for Jade's hand, encasing it in her own. They listened as the gunman made each person walk toward the front of the bus after emptying the contents of their purses or pockets into the box. The bus driver and the armed woman climbed off the bus, and she ordered him to lie facedown in a ditch. Then the others were forced off the bus and into the ditch.

When the gunman reached their row, Banty dumped her satchel's belongings into the box, and Jade emptied her purse. Then he grabbed Jade's hand and pulled off her wedding rings.

"Okay, old lady, give me yours," he ordered.

Banty hadn't taken off her rings for almost fifty years—ever since Wendell had slipped them on her finger. She wasn't sure she could remove them. After several shaky attempts, the rings came off and were added to the madman's collection.

Then Jade and Bandy were ordered to join the others in the ditch. As they stepped off the bus, the sudden burst of night air hit Windsong's face, and she began to cry.

"Shut her up," the woman commanded.

Headlights appeared in the distance, and, as the vehicle came closer, the driver honked his horn repeatedly as some kind of signal to the armed robbers.

Jade pulled Windsong close and whispered lovingly in her ear as she patted the baby, but Windsong would not be quieted. The woman walked over to where Jade was sitting in the ditch and screamed, "If you don't shut her up, I will!" Then, lifting her gun, she pointed it at the innocent child and the pleading young mother.

Banty, knowing she had to do something before this woman hurt Windsong, leapt toward the robber, throwing a handful of dirt and pebbles in her face. The gun discharged into the night air, and Banty was knocked back into the ditch by the blast. The robber cursed and ran for the car to join her companion, who already was in the getaway vehicle.

As the car sped off, people encircled Banty. Jade was screaming hysterically. A young man tried to assure Jade she was no longer in danger. The bus driver knelt down next to Banty, and she opened her eyes.

"How bad is it?" she asked in a halting voice.

The bus driver shone a small flashlight down the front of her sweater until he saw the powder burns. Then, carefully lifting her sweater, he looked to see the extent of her wounds, but he could find no point of entry. When he pulled back her sweater, he noticed something sticking up from her pocket, and he slipped it out. It was her Bible. Stuck in between Jude and Revelation was the bullet.

He helped the rattled Banty to sit up so Jade could see she was alive. Jade fell into Banty's arms, sobbing. For the next half-hour, while they waited for help to reach them, Banty held Jade and Windsong. The reporters, who always seem to know where the next story is, arrived just after the police. A photographer snapped pictures of the three of them rocking in the ditch: one infant wrapped in swaddling clothes; one teenage, tattooed mother; and one wispy-haired old woman.

Later, while Banty was being checked over at the hospital, she remembered her prayer: "Lord, please don't let any unsavory person sit next to me.

I need Your protection. Help me to get home safely. Amen." And she realized He had answered her—in His own way.

Before leaving the hospital, Banty stopped to say good-bye to Jade and Windsong, who were also being examined.

"Mrs. McCluster," the teary-eyed Jade said, "you will stay in touch, won't you?"

"Yes, honey, I will," Banty promised, stroking Windsong's cheek.

After exchanging addresses and telephone numbers, the two women from different worlds embraced. Then Banty turned to leave. "Jade," she said, pausing with her hand on the doorknob.

"Yes, Mrs. McCluster?"

"You may call me Banty."

On the bus ride to her Indiana home, Banty had time to reflect. The problems she had encountered at her son's were not just about Mark and his family, she realized. She had allowed her grief to color her reactions and perceptions.

By the time Banty arrived at her home in Indiana, she had figured out that, yes, the boys were headstrong and her son was argumentative, but then she remembered that the apple doesn't fall far from the tree.

ALL THAT JAZZ

Oh, my heavens! Oh my! Yes! Oh, heavens!" Thirty-six-year-old Nichole Adams waved an envelope in the air as she squealed repeatedly. "Oh, dear! Yes! Yes! Yes!"

A neighbor, Mrs. Winters, who in the act of retrieving her mail heard Nichole's exclamations, hurried across the road to see if Nichole had won the lottery. Quiet, predictable, staid Nichole grabbed Mrs. Winters's hands and began to dance around in circles, dragging the baffled Mrs. Winters with her.

"Are you daft, girl?" Mrs. Winters asked half in jest.

"Yes, yes, deliriously, deliciously daft!"

"Have you gone and won the Irish Sweepstakes?"

"Oh no, much better. I've won a future!" Then, hugging the amazed neighbor, Nichole half waltzed, half jitterbugged her way up the steps and into her living room. She twirled around and around, finally falling backwards into an overstuffed yellow chair. The flowered fabric billowed up as she sank deep into the cushions.

"Thank You, Lord! I will have a life; one filled with interest, people, and challenge. Thank You! Thank You! Thank You!" Too excited to stay seated, Nichole flitted around the house.

"Okay, now let's see. Uh, what should I do first? I know, I'll pack. No, I'd better write my resignation. No, no, I'd better call Mom." Reaching for her cordless, Nichole punched in the familiar numbers. "C'mon, Mom, hurry up. Answer." Nichole paced.

"Hel-lo," her mom answered in her usual, singsong way.

"Mom, it's me. Guess what? It happened! The folks in Chicago have accepted my offer. The store is mine! I'm so jazzed."

"'Jazzed,' Nichole?"

"Happy, Mom, happy!" she almost shouted jubilantly.

"I'm pleased for you, but you sound so, uh, lively."

Nichole burst into laughter. "Yes, Mom, 'lively' fits. I have to go, but I'll call you later. And, Mom, don't worry; I'll come back for visits, I promise."

Nichole was about to fly the coop. Through the years she often had felt like a wounded bird whose wing would not heal, keeping her caged in the confines of her ordinary existence. Born and raised in Livingston County in the small town of Pinckney, Michigan, Nichole had never married, and because of her father's extended illness, then her mom's subsequent struggles, Nichole hadn't felt she could venture off. Following high school graduation she had taken a position in the Howell City Library ten miles from her hometown, and she continued working there for the next eighteen years... that is, until the letter arrived.

She found Pinckney cozy enough. Everyone knew the store owners by their first names, and people still closed off their streets and had neighborhood parties for which the children decorated their bicycles and held parades. Nichole could walk to her mom's down maple-lined streets, and did so at least three times a week. The two of them would sit on her mom's wraparound porch in the summer and dine on salads and shortcakes as they listened to the neighborhood children play hopscotch and tag. In the blustery winter they would sip soup and tea in front of the fireplace while they watched *Jeopardy*. Sunday mornings Nichole and her mom—both blue-eyed and blonde—could be found sitting like matching figurines, one a little more worn than the other, in the third pew from the front on the left-hand side at the First Presbyterian Church. Tuesday evenings Nichole attended a Bible class with eight other women who were all older than she was. Nichole had a tidy life full of the expected. But no more, for Nichole was about to become a notable—no, a prominent—store owner in the bustling Windy City.

She had seen the ad in the *Chicago Tribune* when it arrived at the library six weeks ago: *For sale, antique shop, inventory included, apartment in back of store, good location.* When she read the ad, her heart began to flutter with excitement, and she immediately called to ask for additional information. The owner faxed to the library five pages of the store's inventory as well as photographs of the store and apartment. The photos were a bit obscure, but Nichole could make out enough to know this was what she wanted. She thought about flying over to Chicago to be sure, but her heart told her this was the answer to add dazzle to her predictable life, and she dare not delay in responding lest the opportunity disappear. This was the biggest risk Nichole had ever taken, and she felt as though she might burst from the thrill of it all.

Then, during one of her final days at the library, Nichole was returning some books to their proper place on the shelves in a narrow aisle. She recognized one of her coworkers' voices in the next aisle. "I give Nichole two months. She's too timid to handle the intensity and falderal of the city."

"Oh, she might make it for, say, six months tops," clucked another woman's voice that Nichole recognized but couldn't place. "No, make that three. Winter's coming, and the Windy City, with its gusty ways, is sure to send her packing."

Nichole was a little offended at their lack of confidence in her, and yet, if she were honest, during insecure moments she wondered herself how she would fare. Despite her misgivings and how dramatic the change was, she had pined for just this sort of adventure, and she was determined to follow her heart.

The library put on a festive going-away party for her, which even the Howell mayor attended. He was an avid reader, and Nichole had kept him well informed on the latest releases through the years. She was touched as 126 friends, coworkers, and community constituents gathered to acknowledge her valuable, steady contribution. Even the Chamber of Commerce sent a representative.

Nichole's neighborhood declared "Nichole Day," roped off the streets, and dragged out the barbecues. The children had a "dress up your pet" contest, and Nichole was the presiding judge. The lemonade, root beer, and iced tea flowed freely as music, amplified through the new, deluxe speakers Ted Render had bought from Sears, filled the street with sounds from the fifties. The parents did the swing while the children guffawed in amusement.

But the most emotional parting was with her mom and her best friend, Betsy. The three of them celebrated Nichole's departure by having a private garden party at her mom's. As her mother's health had improved, so had the now-thriving garden. Black-eyed Susans surrounded the yard's perimeter with cheer, as if to announce Nichole's good fortune, while the hydrangea bushes, nestled near the back, formed soft hedges between the neighbors' properties, insuring the threesome a sequestered nook. The red geraniums had sprung back to life after the last cold snap, and Nichole's mom had surrounded them with lobelia, which was having a vibrant second showing.

Over sips of blackberry tea, they spoke of their excitement for Nichole's move, but before the afternoon was over, tears intermingled with the steamy brew. By the time Nichole returned to her house, she was suffering severe pangs of indecision. But by morning she had once again set her face like flint in the direction of her new life.

The one concession Nichole had granted her mom was to agree not to sell her home in Pinckney for one year. "Insurance," her mother called it. Then added, "One never knows, dear, how one's heart might change direction."

Nichole thought keeping the house wouldn't be necessary, but it would help to soothe her mother's grief at least for a while until her mom adjusted to Nichole's absence. Besides, she didn't want to take her furniture until she saw if it suited the apartment. Nichole had rented a hotel room across the street from her shop for the first week until she settled in her place.

So she loaded up her green '95 Cavalier with personal belongings, a few small antiques to add to her store—Victrola, records, teapots, etc.—and headed west. According to her map, if she didn't stop, it would take her about five hours to reach downtown Chicago.

Nichole had been in Chicago ten years earlier for a librarians' weekend convention, but she had traveled in a chartered bus, so this was her first road trip to the area. She felt intimidated by all the semitrucks on Interstate 94, and she hadn't anticipated that the traffic would be so heavy at only two in the afternoon. By the time she reached the downtown area, all vehicles had come to a standstill. She was unaccustomed to such a convergence of traffic and felt twinges of claustrophobia.

It took her an additional hour to reach her exit, which was in eyeshot from where she sat for that hour. Finally, though, she inched forward and was able to zip off her exit and head for her new home and business. It was located in the center of the block on Dearborn between Harrison and Congress. But when she found it, no on-street parking was available nearby. After locating an out-of-the-way spot to park, with an armload of belongings, she excitedly hiked back to her shop.

She noted that the window display featured mostly dust, but she knew in no time she would have the place looking darling. Turning the key, she opened the door and stepped into her very own antique kingdom.

Nichole's eyes widened as she tried to take in her surroundings. The store was a labyrinth with passageways designed out of layers and layers of stuff. While she could identify some of the things, she couldn't imagine why anyone would want them. On one aisle she saw a silver sugar bowl minus the lid, a lamp without a shade, a damaged frame, a butter churn minus the paddle, a bushel basket of rusty tools, a two-foot stack of old magazines, a box of spider-web-covered Mason jars, a plastic radio, a cigar box of dirty prisms, an array of dishes peppered with mouse droppings, and a wooden wagon wheel missing some spokes.

Turning the corner, she spotted a door in the back that she figured would lead into her apartment. She had to push a ladder-back chair to one side, drag a rolled-up rug out of the way, and set aside a child's rickety highchair to reach the door.

When she swung it open, she let out a scream. No sooner did she scream then she began to laugh, and then she burst into tears. There, standing in the doorway looking back at Nichole, was a dingy, six-foot, one-armed, wooden cigar store Indian in full headdress regalia. She backed away, sank into a nearby chair, and had a good cry.

Then, rising up, she announced to the store, "Okay, now I've got that out of my system. You aren't quite what I expected, but you will be. With some ingenuity and tons of elbow grease, we'll become friends in no time." She looked back at the Indian. "And you will be the store sentinel, Chief Broken Wing. Yes, that works. Broken Wing. Tomorrow I'll drag you out of your jail and let you stand guard over my treasure trove. For now, Chief, I'm out of here, but take heart; I will return."

Nichole decided to check into her hotel room across the street. But as she stepped outside the shop, she was accosted by the Chicago winds, which sent her baseball cap sailing into the street. Before she could rescue it, a cab flattened the cap, leaving greasy tread marks across the crushed bill. Fighting to stay upright as the wind circled around her, Nichole made her way over to the safety of the hotel lobby.

By 6 A.M. she was up, dressed in jeans and her Red Wings sweatshirt, and ready to tackle her day. Notepad in hand she roamed the store, jotting down supplies she would need: window cleaner, broom, mousetraps, dust pan, vacuum cleaner, hammer, nails, screwdriver, paint, brushes, mousetraps, roller, stepladder, soap, furniture polish, room spray, mousetraps, and gallons of disinfectant. Then she headed for Chief Broken Wing and her apartment.

The Chief was awkward to pull out, but he wasn't as heavy as she had feared. Once he was positioned by the checkout counter, she was ready to tour her new home. Stepping inside her living quarters, she realized *tour* was a generous word for such a brief floor plan. It was four rooms if you counted the closet, which she decided to do. The largest room was the living room–kitchen; the bedroom was modest, but the bath was surprisingly generous and included an enormous footed-tub and a marble sink. The closet was a walk-in—that is, if you ducked, because the ceiling slanted inside, making maneuvering a bit of a challenge. The windows in the living room, bedroom, and bath all looked out on the alley and her back-door neighbor's commercial garbage receptacles. That was a bit of a jolt, but Nichole was determined to maintain a positive attitude.

After getting lost several times trying to learn her way around town, Nichole finally located the stores and supplies she needed and headed back to her shop. Prices were higher in the city than she was used to, but she had known that would probably be so. Her goal for the day was to clean her apartment and move in as soon as possible. Exaggerated prices weren't going to diminish her energy.

She rolled up her sleeves and methodically began to scrub and sweep. By two o'clock, she realized she would have to stop for lunch. Remembering she had spotted a Starbucks on the corner, she ran down to grab a latté and a salad.

When she finished eating, Nichole longed for a nap, but she wasn't about to give in to her weariness with all she had to do. She laughed to herself, thinking librarians weren't used to such aerobic feats as battling wind gusts and wrestling with Indian chiefs.

Much to her delight, Nichole was able to borrow a few things from her store to minimally decorate the apartment. She dragged in a club chair for the living room and a small vanity table and a mismatched padded stool for the bathroom. A narrow wooden table with two odd chairs became her eating space and desk. She was grateful that both an apartment-sized refrigerator and a stove resided in the galley kitchen. Two of the stove's burners worked, and the fridge, after a brutal scrubbing, was able to store food safely. The kitchen faucet had an annoying leak that she would need to fix, but she would tend to that tomorrow. All she needed now was a bed.

Nichole leaned over to the Chief and lamented, "Bed. Yes, all I need is a bed. Hey, partner, how about giving me the rest of the night off? I'm beat." It was almost six o'clock, so Nichole locked up the store, ordered a small pizza to go from the pizza parlor two doors down, and headed to the hotel.

By the time she arrived in her room, she fell face forward on the bed, promising herself she would get right up. At 3:30 A.M. she awoke disoriented. After shaking her mental cobwebs enough to function, she quickly slid out of her clothes and into the bed. By 5:30 she was up, showered, dressed, and on her way out the door. She grabbed the pizza box and decided her neglected dinner would work for breakfast and lunch today.

"Hi, Chief Broken Wing," Nichole called as she opened the store door. "It's a new day."

She set her pizza on the counter next to the chief and spotted water trickling from under the apartment door down the store aisle. "Oh no," she cried out as she ran to the back and entered the living room. She sloshed her way over to the sink and fished a scouring pad out of the blocked drain, which had caused the sink to flood over.

Nichole grabbed some towels from a bag she had brought from home and began to sponge up the water. Two hours later, her back aching, she finally squeezed out the last sopping towels.

"Chief, I'm docking your wages. Surely you must have realized your moccasins were getting wet," Nichole chided, as she sat on the countertop munching cold pizza.

Banging on the front door interrupted her conversation. "Oh good. It's the telephone man."

An hour later she had a phone, and she immediately called Betsy and her mom to give them her new number and to whine about her flood. Two hours after that the mattress and box springs she had ordered arrived, and Nichole had to talk fast and tip big to get the deliveryman to take the mattress and springs to the bedroom all the way in the back. She just knew her anatomy wouldn't hold up to dragging them herself, especially after she had already mopped up half the Chicago River.

Nichole didn't have a bedframe but figured she could make do for now. She didn't mind sleeping on the floor as long as no critters were scampering about in the night. She already had trapped six mice in the last two days and figured she had cleared the place. To make sure the store was truly de-moused, Nichole decided to sleep one more night at the hotel. If the traps were empty tomorrow, she would officially move in.

Leaning against her Indian comrade, she asked, "What do you think I should tackle next, Chief-y?"

The longer she looked around, the more overwhelmed she felt until finally tears began to slip down her face. Oh, how Nichole wished her mom and Betsy were with her. They would know how to advise her.

Rapping on the front window grabbed Nichole's attention, and she quickly dabbed at her tears with her sweatshirt sleeves. Standing outside was a brunette woman with a big smile and a vase full of purple and pink hydrangeas. Nichole opened the door to a perky greeting.

"Hi, neighbor. Welcome to the block. I'm Jana, and I own the flower shop next door. You have a quite a challenge here. I thought these flowers might add a little cheer to your day. They do mine. That's why I opened my shop: to add some cheer and color to people's lives. Of course, making a liv-ing wouldn't hurt my feelings either." She laughed. "I thought just moving in and all you might not have unpacked a vase, so you can use mine. No rush to return it." Jana was backing out the door, even as she spoke.

The woman's presence felt like a hug to Nichole. "Thanks, Jana. By the way, I'm Nichole, and these flowers couldn't have come at a better time." Her voice started to break. Embarrassed, she gave a quick wave and stepped back into her store to tend to her leaky eyes.

"Chief, don't take this personally," Nichole said with a sniff, "but hav-ing someone to talk to who isn't wearing wooden feathers and doesn't smoke cigars was kind of nice, if only for a minute."

She set the vase in the window and then decided, after stepping back and viewing it, that the window was where she would focus her attention. She cleaned the showcase glass inside and out, vacuumed the floor, and scrubbed the ledges. Next she selected to feature in the window some of the nicer items she gradually was unearthing. An oak hat stand had polished up nicely, and Nichole hung from the hooks a black Stetson and a woman's fussy, red-plumed, yellow felt hat. Next to the stand she placed a red velvet upholstered rocker with oak arms shaped like lions' heads. Close to the rocker she nestled an oval table draped with a floor-length crocheted covering. She topped that with a large oil lamp and an 1894 leather-covered hymnal. To accent the décor, Nichole placed a hand-stitched pillow on the chair and a hooked rug on the floor. Then she set a copper pail in the corner that she hoped to fill with poplar logs to give the look of a cozy place to nestle for the coming winter.

Nichole admired the results of her efforts from several angles and felt encouraged. Then she turned and looked at the work looming throughout the rest of the shop, and her mood dropped. As her eyes moved from wall to wall, she noticed once again the flowers from Jana. Walking over to the vase, Nichole touched the beautiful blue and mauve hydrangeas. She couldn't help but think of home. Home, where life was orderly and predictable and cigar-store Indians weren't hovering behind doors.

"Snap out of it," Nichole admonished herself aloud. "For heaven's sake, the Chief here is going to think you're a homesick camper instead of the sophisticated entrepreneur you are." Then, in her best librarian's voice, she instructed, "Nichole, girl, you're talking to a wooden statue; call it a night. Night, Chief."

When Nichole was halfway across the street to the hotel, a man on the curb pointed in her direction and screamed, "The world is coming to an end! Repent, sinner!"

Nichole, unaccustomed to street people, did a pivot, and, shaking, headed back toward the store.

"Leave her alone, Preacher," a voice shouted at the man. "Go save the sinners on Harrison, or I won't give you any more pizza."

The preacher man scowled at the sidewalk and then hurried off, his hat pulled down to his eyebrows and his hands buried in his overcoat pockets.

Nichole looked down toward the pizza parlor where a heavyset, balding man, who was clearing the sidewalk tables, smiled and waved. "It's okay. He's harmless, just loud."

"Thank you." Nichole sighed and again changed directions, making a quick path to the hotel. She learned from the doorman that a block away was a homeless shelter, and she prepared herself for the possibility, in the days ahead, of encountering quite an array of socially forgotten folks.

Once inside her room she slid into a steaming bath and hoped the warmth would relieve her aching muscles. Afterwards she checked in with Betsy and her mom by phone to give them the latest progress report.

By 10:00 P.M. Nichole was sound asleep. She dreamed that Chief Broken Wing was sitting in the rocker in the store window wearing the sidewalk preacher's coat, drinking a Starbucks coffee, and laughing his headdress off. In the morning Nichole decided, based on her dream, that city life was making her ditsy.

When she arrived at her shop door, she had two customers waiting for her—Jana from the flower shop and a man. "Hi, Nichole," Jana said. "This is my husband, Brett. We have two hours to give you before our shop opens. We're great helpers; just point us in a direction and watch us do our thing."

"Oh my." Nichole fumbled for the key and for words. "I...I don't know what to say."

"You don't have to say a thing. We understand how wild it can be trying to get things in place," Brett said. His smile was as welcoming as Jana's. Brett towered over his perky wife; yet his gentle nature made him approachable.

Nichole assigned the first pile of junk to Jana to go through and see what was salvageable while Brett was assigned the leaky faucet in the apartment. Nichole headed for a china cabinet that was loaded with assorted items to determine their condition and value.

Jana was delighted with her task, oohing and aahing as she worked.

When she discovered the box of prisms, she headed to the back to find a pail and soap. A short time later she emerged tickled with how well they had cleaned up. She strung them on a fishing line and hung them in the window. As the sunlight touched them, tiny rainbows began to flicker about the room. Jana and Nichole applauded. Brett stuck his head out the apartment door to see what was going on. "Oh, I get it, it's a girl thing."

By the time Brett and Jana had to leave, Nichole was encouraged. "Thank you both so much. Could I treat the two of you to dinner sometime?"

"Sure, how about tonight?" Jana laughed. "No, no, I'm just teasing."

They laughed together with such ease that Nichole knew they would be friends.

Brett said, "How about after our shop closes at 5:30 we pick up some pizza and the three of us eat here? I think we could put in another hour or two to help get this place shipshape, don't you, Jana?"

"Works for me, big boy," she quipped. "See you later, Nichole."

The hours flew by as Nichole moved about the store restoring order. In fact, when Jana tapped on the door, the sound startled Nichole. She couldn't believe they were back already.

After the trio ate, they worked until 9:15 before they took inventory on their progress. They were quite impressed with themselves and took turns patting each other on the back.

"Is there anything else we can help you with before we leave?" Brett inquired.

"Well, since you asked, yes, there is. Brett, would you mind checking my mousetraps? I meant to do it earlier, but now that it's nighttime, I'm kind of a coward."

"Sure, where are they?"

Nichole directed him to the trap sites, and to her dismay Brett found three new victims.

"Oh, yuck. It's back to the hotel for me."

Nichole started to trudge across the street, weary from the long day, and stepped into a car's path. The driver lay on the horn as he swerved to miss her, and then he screeched to a stop, opened his window, and filled the air with his rage. Nichole was stunned and offended yet grateful she hadn't become an ornament on the guy's hood. She chastised herself for not being more cautious while wanting to bean the driver for not being more understanding. She still hadn't adjusted to the city's heavy traffic or the short fuses it seemed to generate.

Once in the safety of her room, the shaken Nichole called Betsy to help settle herself down. Just hearing Betsy's voice brought such a sense of relief. The two chattered for an hour about their respective days, then the childhood friends ended their visit with wish-you-were-here's.

Over the next week the store began to take on a distinct personality, and since Nichole was so close to being done, she left the front door open for the curious. At first, area folks stopped by to see how things had shaped up, but then gradually people began to make purchases. In fact, one lady, Sadie Wilkins, who had just moved into an apartment on the street, bought an oak buffet, a small lady's secretary, and a framed Dutch print. Then a sixty-year-old, silver-haired gentleman shocked her when he walked into the store and announced he wanted to buy the window.

"Excuse me?" Nichole asked.

"I'd like to buy the display of things you have in your window," he repeated.

"All of the things?"

"Yes. I'm a widower starting over again, and I realized after I rented a place across the street that I really don't know how to begin anew. Then I saw your charming window, and I thought, 'Okay, I'll begin here.' Do you think that absurd?"

"Oh no, sir, not absurd; I just was surprised to have a request for all of it. I think you're quite brave to start on a new journey."

"Brave? No, not at all. I was married to my wife, Rachel, for forty years, and when she died, my dreams died with her. I'm just biding time now." He cleared his throat to cover the emotion that seemed to have caught him off guard. "And I thought I could bide time sitting in that rocker."

"Why don't you describe your apartment to me, and perhaps I could make a few suggestions?" Nichole offered.

After their initial meeting, the gentleman, Cliffton Jeffries, became a regular customer and sometimes even a part-time employee, assisting with minor repairs. Best of all, though, he became Nichole's friend. In fact, Nichole introduced him to Sadie Wilkins, the lady who had bought the oak buffet, and the two soon developed into a neighborhood item. They had been spotted rendezvousing at the pizza parlor, and Cliffton had been seen purchasing small bouquets of roses from Jana.

Sometimes Sadie and Cliffton would offer to watch the store to give Nichole a break. She might run errands or search for inventory for the shop, but usually, when given the opportunity, Nichole would hang out at the library. Even though it was five times larger than the library she had worked at, the place flooded her with wonderful memories. She would finger old books' bindings, smell the leather, and sit and admire the endless selection of literature, history, science, and the arts. Often Nichole would draw off the shelf the works of Winslow Homer, delighting in his depictions of country living and fishing in forgotten streams. She also would linger over Georgia O'Keeffe's books of flowers, tracing the petals with her mind. When she would leave the library, an unexplained forlornness would follow her back to the store.

One evening after work in late January, after making it through the financially lucrative, exhausting holidays, Nichole was rummaging through some boxes of eclectic finds. She came across an old Indian blanket, probably for a horse saddle, and draped it over Chief Broken Wing's shoulder to cover his missing arm. It gave him the appearance of being whole.

"Chief, that blanket might make you look better, but we both know your arm is still missing." She was surprised to find tears forming in her eyes as she spoke. She realized Chief Broken Wing wasn't the only one missing something vital. She had overcome so many obstacles to see her dream come true, but now she understood she had been pushing an important truth down beneath the surface of realization. What she really wanted was to be a librarian in Howell, Michigan. She wanted to visit her mom weekly, pick out books for the mayor, have tea with Betsy, and lead a small-town life filled with quiet pleasures. It wasn't that she hadn't made friends, or that the business wasn't doing well, but she was more suited to peaceful over bustling, to family over activity, to books over antiques, to simple over all the jazz she had thought she needed to make life textured.

"Now what am I going to do, Chief?"

The next few days were difficult for Nichole as she battled within herself. She didn't want to be a quitter, and she didn't want to look like a failure. Then, on Thursday, Nichole was relieved to see Cliffton walk through her front door. She realized the years and his losses had given him a sense of people, and she needed a wise friend right now. Nichole confessed her dilemma to him.

"Change always takes courage," Cliffton said. "Remember what you called me when we first met? Brave. It was a brave thing you did to take a risk and follow your dream, Nichole. But now, child, you have a greater calling: to find where your heart is at home. If you hadn't come here, you would still be in Pinckney, keeping your life on hold, waiting for your dreams to come true. Sometimes we can't know what we want until we have a way to measure it through other experiences. Now you can return wiser and braver."

Nichole hugged Cliffton and thanked him for his many kindnesses. Then she picked up the phone and placed an ad that read, *For sale. Antique shop. Inventory included (minus cigar-store Indian). Apt. in back. Good location. Great neighbors.* She turned to her Indian friend and said, "You heard the man: you chief, me brave. Let's vamoose."

An offer for the store came sooner than Nichole expected. It seemed a newlywed couple had heard of the sale and thought a business with an apartment would be a great beginning for them. Cliffton and Sadie Jeffries purchased the store on February 14. Cliffton, winking in Nichole's direction, said he knew exactly how to decorate the front window. Two weeks later, with help from Jana and Brett, Nichole lowered the Chief through the sunroof of her car and headed home.

BOXED IN

On my return from town there loomed, like a suspicious intruder, a mound of parcels at my back door. I groaned so loud when I spotted them that my neighbor, who was watering his lawn, called out, "Are you okay, Becky?" I waved my hand to signal my well-being, but under my breath I grumbled my displeasure. A deliveryman had left the pile of boxes while I was off traipsing through the hardware store in search of screws for my collapsing pantry shelf.

As I made my way around and through the cartons, I counted five...six...eight...oh no, ten of them. Ten boxes. That was even worse than I had imagined. Ten boxes of leftovers from a cranky old aunt's life. Actually, she was my great-aunt. Great, what a joke. She was a spiteful woman who had wanted nothing to do with me, and now that she was gone, I was the one saddled with her belongings. Why me? I had enough of my own junk; I didn't need anyone else's. Perhaps I would just put the whole kit and caboodle in a yard sale and be done with it. Hmm, maybe I could sell my house, too, contents included, and then someone else could sort through my stuff and, while that person was at it, repair the lopsided pantry shelf.

After plopping my purse, keys, and bag on the kitchen counter, I headed for the flashing answering machine. Pen in hand, I listened as Phil, my husband, reported that he had made it safely to Vancouver and that he wished I was with him this weekend. "Sure," I retorted, "and just who would take care of the kids, repair the shelf, and deal with Aunt Virginia's boxes?"

I decided a cup of tea might help settle me down because obviously I wasn't having a good day—or week, for that matter. I put on the kettle and sat down to sort through some unopened mail. Same old stuff: junk mail, credit-card applications, bills…and a letter.

My attention turned to the letter. The return address was from the same town in Kentucky where my aunt had lived, but I was unfamiliar with the person's name. I opened the envelope and read.

Dear Mrs. Rebecca Hansen,

I was a friend of your aunt's. Well, friend might be a stretch since, as you know, she wasn't given to friendliness. Yet Virginia and I visited a number of times over the past six months, as I needed information she had that she measured out sparingly to me. Perhaps she knew her life's end was near and that was the reason she let someone into her tight circle.

I believe your aunt to have been an embittered but brilliant woman. She was certainly complex; yet I found myself drawn to something within her that was…how shall I say…"dear."

Your Aunt Virginia had been friends with my great-grandfather, who passed away when I was very young. I was in search of information about him when someone suggested I talk to your aunt, who grew up in the same neighborhood as my great-grandfather. At first Virginia was almost hostile when I phoned her, but after several more attempts I noticed she softened. So one day I showed up at her door, and she let me in. That was the beginning of our relationship.

Since Virginia did not have the interior freedom to relate with you while she was living, I want to encourage you to meet your great-aunt now through her belongings. When Virginia spoke of you, she was obviously regretful that she had shut you out. Even though she was a wounded soul, she was a worthwhile one. I'm so sorry she didn't know that sooner. Yes, I watched in the last weeks of her life as she relinquished her anger and a quietness rested upon her. How sad that she lived in anguish, but how wonderful that she died in relative peace.

I know you received a letter from the court telling you of your inheritance. I packed up your boxes at Virginia's request, and I think you might be surprised at their contents. Her furnishings were auctioned off per her instruction, and the money paid for her funeral expenses and resolved a few small debts. The remainder was donated to a local charity for the homeless.

What I would have given to have a tangible box of my great-grandfather's belongings! All I have are my little girl's shadowy memories. Forgive me if this letter is intrusive; that was not my desire.

If you should ever want to reach me my name is

Eleanor Williams
1652 Meyers Rd.
Littleton, Kentucky

The screeching kettle redirected my attention. I dropped the letter onto the stack of mail, grabbed a hot pad, and pulled the steaming kettle off the burner.

After I filled my cup, I headed back to the letter and reread Eleanor Williams's words: "friend"…"dear"…"wounded soul"…"died in peace." I was stunned and moved. I had learned more about my aunt from a stranger's letter than I had ever known. I just had considered Aunt Virginia a wretched old relative too ornery to bother with…end of story. Even other relatives, now deceased, had warned me to stay away from her, and I pretty much had heeded their advice. Since I lived in Ohio and Aunt Virginia in Kentucky, it was easy not to even give her a thought. I wasn't pleased when the letter from the court regarding my inheritance had arrived. I'm not certain why, but I had found it unsettling.

Now I pulled the various boxes inside the kitchen and stacked them out of the flow of my sons, who would soon thunder through the door like Niagara Falls. Glen, Jimmy, Billy, and Jay were rambunctious renegades who kept me bellowing and blessed. I was grateful it was Friday, and my tribe would be picked up by my husband's niece, Carol, and her husband, Bruce, who had bravely offered to take the boys camping. I had their clothes sorted and packed along with enough treats to feed a Boy Scout troop. And I had assembled a box bulging with bug spray, sunscreen, a first-aid kit, extra Band-Aids, batteries, and assorted flashlights. *Watch out, woods* was all I could think, as I envisioned my sons being released into the wild.

The boys rushed in the door, just as I knew they would. Then, just as rapidly, each boy was properly threatened and warmly hugged, and their departure was accomplished.

I headed back in the house to deal with the broken shelf and a growing curiosity about the boxes. I decided to open one box and then head into the pantry for the repair work. But which box should I start with?

I shuffled a few around, and then I noticed they were numbered in the lower left-hand corner. I wasn't sure if that information was for me or the delivery company, but I decided to start with number one.

After locating it, I dragged it in front of an overstuffed chair. Inside was a packing list that simply said, "Contents from Front Closet."

"Oh no, don't tell me they sent her clothes?" Reluctantly I pulled back the paper to uncover a set of china. The pattern was old, yet the pieces appeared unused. I turned one plate over, and on the underside it read "Limoges." The delicate rose pattern was pleasing, and the set was extensive. In fact, box number two held the rest of the dishes, making it a service for eight that included several lovely serving bowls.

The fine china didn't seem to fit my aunt's rough exterior or her limited resources. From what I could tell and from what I had heard, she had lived a modest life. I didn't understand why she would have these lovely yet apparently unused dishes. These were definitely not yard-sale material, but I wasn't certain I could eat off dishes that belonged to someone who could never be bothered with me.

I started for the pantry, but the next thing I knew I was pulling box number three over to be opened. The packing list in this one stated, "Contents from Boxes Under Bed." I hesitated. *What would a woman like her stash under her bed? An Uzi?* I giggled to myself.

Inside I found three quilts and a tin. The quilts were handmade and, like the china, were unused. The workmanship was exquisite with each stitch perfectly executed. The tin held thread, scraps of material, and a pair of scissors with the name "Virginia" etched into the handle. Then I noticed a paper tucked under the thread. I fished it out and opened a note hand-written in impeccable script.

For you, my dear, I sewed each stitch
Your life and love have made me rich.
Wrapped in the warmth of yesterdays
We'll share tomorrow always.

Gina

"Gina?" Could that possibly have been something my Aunt Virginia wrote to someone? I couldn't imagine my aunt in love, or even young, for that matter. And I had never heard anyone call her Gina. I took the quilts and spread them across the couch. With my eyes and fingers I scanned them, as if searching for answers to my questions. In the lower corner of each quilt were the initials "G. W." What was Virginia Owens doing with G. W.'s quilts?

I walked over to the remaining boxes and searched out number four. It was beginning to split at the corners from the weight inside. I carefully dragged it across the room. Inside this box was another box and a packing slip that stated, "Contents from Storage Bin."

Layers of wrapping paper and bubble wrap were wound around four items of varying sizes. The first was an etched, ruby glass basket in a sterling stand that I placed on the end table. My breath caught in my throat as the sunlight from the window illuminated its beauty. Such elegance from such a dismal person.

Carefully I removed a weighty cylindrical package encased in bubble wrap and newspaper. I peeled off the layers to find the base of an elaborate lamp made from scrolled iron with a solid marble stem. The next paper parcel held the hand-painted globe, and the smaller package held the chimney. I fit the lamp pieces together and then stood back to look at it assembled. The choice banquet lamp stood about twenty-four inches high. Once again the beauty and condition of the piece were impeccable.

I realized that these items were valuable and that I could probably sell them for a hefty sum. Why did my aunt have such a trove of lovely items, why did they appear unused, and why did she leave them to me, someone she had refused to even speak with? Why didn't she just have them auctioned off with her furnishings?

I had tried several times through the years to acknowledge her. I had sent a couple of notes, and one year I even had sent her a birthday card. My aunt did respond to the card with a curt postcard asking me not to send any more mail. So I didn't. Now I wondered, what if I had persisted...

I decided to stop and eat to escape my uncomfortable feelings and my undeserved inheritance. Rummaging around in the fridge, I settled on last night's leftovers of vegetable lasagna, a hunk of French bread, and a tall glass of lemonade. I carried it to the back porch to avoid the disorder that slowly was overtaking my home. Boxes and packing debris were scattered willy-nilly throughout my kitchen, dining room, and living room. I felt a little strange having the belongings of someone I barely knew strewn about.

Actually, it seemed odd to have my home to myself. Usually on the weekends my sons filled these rooms with their playful presence and pesky persistence. And, before a weekend was over, Phil invariably organized a family ball game in the backyard and insisted I be the umpire. What a fiasco! What a joy! I loved the five frisky men in my life.

Soon my thoughts trailed back to the boxes and my Aunt Virginia. I wondered what my aunt would have thought of my family. I couldn't imagine that our boys wouldn't have warmed her cold heart with their endearing ways. But it was too late to wonder, and I tried to move away from those thoughts.

I set my dishes in the sink, and then I grabbed a new carton to open. The packing list read, "Addl. Contents Storage Bin."

The box held a modest trunk about the size of a large hatbox. The tin, brocade-patterned sides were held together with scrolled hinges. The top was curved and had a worn leather clasp that held it closed. As I opened the trunk, the musty smell of days long ago slipped out and encircled me. The lid was lined in a faded calico print with aged ribbons that held a small shelf in place. The shelf had three tissue-wrapped items: a sterling silver brush, comb, and hand mirror. I turned them over in my hands, admiring their tarnished beauty. These would polish into a treasured vanity set.

Under the shelf was a locked wooden box. Taped on top was a note from Eleanor Williams.

> I couldn't find the key for this lock. When I asked your aunt just
> a few days before her death about the key, she whispered some-
> thing about its being behind the steps. I checked everywhere I
> could think of without success.
>
> Eleanor

I lifted the carved box out of its nest and examined the tiny lock. It wouldn't take much to break it, but I hated to risk harming the intricate box. Finally, after a careful examination, I decided to set it aside and open the next carton.

Boxes number six and seven were books. Wonderful books. They included handsome leather editions of Charles Dickens's classics from the

1800s, a lovely book of sonnets by Elizabeth Barrett Browning, and ten volumes of Jane Austen's work.

I was so thrilled, my heart was skipping beats. Obviously the books had been read and reread; yet they were all intact and well maintained. In the front of each was an inscription that read, "To our darling Virginia. With love, Grandma Grace & Grandpa Milton."

Tears began to trickle down my face. Tears of joy, for I loved books, especially old ones, and I longed to build a library, but with the expenses of young children that just hadn't been a priority. My tears were also from a growing sadness that this distant old aunt had loved some of the same things I did. And even though we lived far apart, we may have been close in heart interests. Strange I had never thought of my spinster aunt as having a heart. She always seemed sealed off to relationships.

Box seven included children's schoolbooks that appeared unused and a three-volume set of nursery rhymes that were quite tattered. A tissue-wrapped school slate in a wooden frame and a small, tin lunchpail were tucked in the box as well. Inside the pail was a photograph of a wisp of a child, her light hair encircling her delicate face and her impish smile. At the bottom of the box was a slender copy of Shakespeare with a handwritten inscription that read, "To Gina, My Juliet—From Your Romeo." There was that name again. Gina.

I stood, turned on the lights to ward off the growing darkness, and stretched out the kinks in my neck. Then I eyed the remaining stack of three boxes. This dreaded chore had turned into guarded joy for me. I was beginning to appreciate that these treasured items were from my family, even if from a cantankerous branch on the family tree.

When I opened the eighth box, the contents page made my heart flutter with excitement. "From Gina's Room."

Ah, finally some answers. I quickly pulled back the tissue and found myself more confused than ever. The box was full of a young child's belongings: dresses, bonnets, crocheted sweaters and coverlets, a rag doll with button eyes, hair ribbons, a framed picture of stone steps that led into a walled garden, and a blanket monogrammed "Gina Dear." Each item had been individually wrapped, although the tissue was crumbling and yellowed from age.

I had heard that my great-aunt, her brother, and their parents had barely escaped with their lives from a house fire when Virginia was twelve, and that they had lost all their belongings. So to whom did these little girl clothes belong?

I slid another box over to investigate, in hopes it would shed some additional light on Gina. This box contained photographs, most without names, and many of the people pictured I didn't recognize. A few were of my aunt, and most of those were when she was a young schoolteacher. In one photo Aunt Virginia was smiling. She looked surprisingly pretty.

Then I did something quite odd; I hugged her picture. I don't know why. Perhaps because, for the first time, she had allowed me into her life, and I needed to reciprocate.

Only one unopened container was left, and it was the smallest. The paper inside box number ten said, "Contents: Deed."

Deed? Why would I be given her deed? I opened the envelope, and, sure enough, inside was the deed for her home. My head became light as I tried to make sense of this unexpected gift. Aunt Virginia's signature validated that the property had been signed over to me with a contingency clause. The clause stated that I would, in trade for the property, financially maintain Virginia and Gina Owens's grave sites.

Now my mind was scampering from one thought to another. Could it be that Gina was my aunt's child? I was out of boxes but certainly not questions. In fact, my unanswered thoughts pressed on my heart.

I glanced up, and my eyes fell on the small locked box. I carried it into the living room and sat in a wing chair. I pulled carefully on the lock, but years of resolve held it in place. Then I gently rocked the box as I tried to listen to its secrets. It sounded like paper and small belongings sliding back and forth. I placed the box in my lap for a moment, leaned back in the chair, and closed my eyes. I began to rummage around in my mind, when suddenly a thought came to me. I headed for the kitchen.

Let's see, it was box number eight. Yes, eight. I reached into the box and pulled out the framed picture of the stone steps. Could it be…yes, yes, taped on the underside was a piece of brown paper covering a small key. Now I was giggling as I rushed back to the box and, with trembling hands, slipped the key into the lock, and the box opened. Inside were my aunt's glasses, letters tied together with ribbons, and some photographs. The pictures were of my aunt and a handsome man in a uniform. I opened a letter addressed to my aunt.

Dear, Dear, Gina,

How I miss you. I dream of you even when I am awake. My commander told me that we will not have to be here long. I will come home soon, and then we shall never be apart again. Promise me that you will wait for me and that when I return we will wed. I am committed to our future.

I glanced down to the bottom of the letter to end my own suspense, and it was signed, "Your Romeo, James." I scanned the envelope and the return address was from Lieutenant James Williams. I counted eleven letters from him over a three-month period. Each letter was tender, but in the later letters, James eluded to a conflict with his family regarding their upcoming marriage. In his final correspondence to my aunt, he wrote that he was unable to "fulfill my promise to marry you. I hope you will forgive me. I know you will find this difficult to believe, but I will always love you."

Tears flooded down my face as I felt my aunt's world fall apart. I realized the lovely items in the boxes were my aunt's hope chest that she could never bear to use.

After dabbing at my eyes with a Kleenex, I reached back in the box and lifted out a certificate. It was a death certificate for a four-year-old child.

Gina. Attached to it was a newspaper clipping that recounted the drowning of young Gina Owens when the boat she was in with her great-grandfather capsized.

That must have broken my aunt's heart. James never mentioned my aunt's pregnancy in his letters, which made me believe she might never have told him. I also discovered some letters that my Aunt Virginia had written to her brother and never mailed, regarding her pregnancy out of wedlock. Before Gina's death, Virginia wrote that she regretted the shame and reproach she had brought upon her family and prayed that they would one day find it in their hearts to forgive her.

Virginia named her daughter Gina in memory of James's nickname for her. Determined to make a life for Gina and herself, my great-aunt moved in with her grandparents. Not long after Gina's death, Virginia's grandfather's health failed, and he passed away. Her grandmother pined over her losses until the following year she, too, died. I suppose that was when my Great-Aunt Virginia emotionally climbed the stone steps and hid in the walled enclosure.

The accumulation of my aunt's losses was almost more than I could bear to take in. I realized now that Aunt Virginia's sullen behavior wasn't about me; it was all about her. She had no space for anyone. She was locked in so much pain, she couldn't reach the key to escape her misery, and none of us knew where it was hidden.

I passed by the counter where Eleanor's letter lay when I realized her last name and James's was the same. As I reread the letter, I knew she had been sent to my great-aunt because Eleanor's great-grandfather was Virginia's beloved James. I knew then what I must do. I took out a pen and paper and began...

Dear Eleanor,

What a day in my life this has been. You encouraged me to
get to know my aunt through her belongings, and truly I have.

My heart aches that I did not have the maturity to move past
Aunt Virginia's resistant ways and befriend her as you did. Thank
you for your important and tender role at the end of her life.

You mentioned your longing to have a tangible way to
remember your great-grandfather, and I believe I can help you
with that. I need to come to your town to settle my aunt's estate.
May we meet? I have some things to share with you that I think
will help you to know your great-grandfather better. And my
findings might help you to understand my aunt's reluctance to
tell you more.

It is hard to believe what a wide circle our lives make, reaching forward and back for generations. And yet we can be con-
densed down to ten boxes of belongings. How small we are and
yet how lasting our influence.

Going through Aunt Virginia's boxes was like putting on her
spectacles and seeing for the first time from her vantage point.
What a painful way to learn. But it has been a lesson I will not
forget.

Gratefully,
Rebecca

I then addressed and stamped the envelope for the morning mail. I
glanced over at the kitchen clock and was amazed to find it was 2:00 A.M.
I stood to go to bed, but I had to do one more thing.

I dug into the bottom drawer until I found a hammer and a nail and
then headed for the pantry. After securing the nail into the door, I hung the
stone step picture to insure I never would forget this day or my dear Aunt
Virginia.

MRS. CASS'S

NEIGHBORLY WAYS

Winnifred Jenkins—known as Winnie to most—has reason to be circumspect. She's being audited. No, not the financial kind that causes one to break out in hives the size of silver dollars. Winnie is being scrutinized by the Sourgum, Virginia, PTA. Yep, this is a biggie for her because we all know how, uh, *selective* a group of concerned citizens can be. And let's face it, Winnie has a reputation of colorful proportions—lime green and fuchsia with shades of vivid violet, I'd say.

Who am I? Winnifred's guardian angel. Well, guardian might be a stretch. Let's just say I give ol' Winnie nudges in the right direction when she's of a mind to be nudged. (I spend a lot of time hanging out with the Maytag repairman.)

I was commissioned to Winnie at her birth, which in itself was no easy assignment. In an athletic moment she decided to enter life by springing out of the chute feet first. This was a tad distressing to her mom, who didn't realize that was just the beginning of Winnifred's pell-mell mind-set. And I, well, I took a deep breath and rolled my eyes heavenward, wondering what I had done to deserve this assignment. God does not explain these things, even to guardian angels.

Winnie bypassed crawling and went right to a boot-scootin' boogie, for this little girl had big plans. And part of her plan was not to allow anyone else's plan to get in the way of hers. Like the day as a toddler, or in her case boogie-woogie dancer, she decided shoes were unnecessary winter attire. She dashed out the door barefooted into eight inches of freshly fallen snow. Her mom, bless her hammering heart, tried to catch Winnie, but she was as determined as a greased pig to escape her mother's clutches.

I hovered over the blue-toed toddler, who was skipping gleefully down the street, as I tried to reason with her. She, of course, wasn't listening. Her fleet-footed father finally caught up with us about a block and a half from home. Three neighbors already had phoned child services before he could get the little ice princess back to the house. Bless those neighbors' concerned hearts.

Winnie's escapades included a fire of sorts, when, at three years of age, she found her uncle's Zippo lighter in the chair cushion and discovered the lovely shower of sparks it created when she twirled the wheel. Her mom dragged the smoldering chair out into the snow where it burst into a lovely bonfire, as did Winnie's miffed mom. Who, by the way, single-handedly doused the fiery chair in snow using the mailbox she had ripped off the side of the house as a pail.

I personally have an aversion to fire and was grateful for the buildup of winter precipitation. For when I had nudged the little spitfire to drop the Zippo, I singed my raiment and therefore found it necessary to stop, drop, and roll. (Mrs. Cass, who lived three houses down, called the fire department after the chair flames were extinguished. Thank you, Mrs. Cass; it's the thought that counts.)

When Winnifred's dad brought home a collie, Winnie was almost delighted. She had wanted a dog for a long time—but she had a French poodle in mind. Winnie always had backup plans for moments like these. So, utilizing all four years of her life experience, Winnie gave Sassie an up close and personal haircut with her mom's pinking shears. Then she gathered the remaining tufts and tied them with pink ribbons. To say Mom was surprised when Winnie promenaded Sassie up and down the street would be to underestimate the moment. In fact, Winnie's mom did a pit-bull growl in Winnie's direction that would have scared a, uh, pit bull.

To extend the quality of the little dog groomer's life, that time I nudged her mom. Well, actually I passed an old memory across the screen of her mom's mind. When she was seven years old, in her desire to be a beautician, she had given her Pekinese, Chop Suey, a permanent, which she had left on too long, causing little Chop Suey to look more like Rice-A-Roni.

(A tip of the hat goes to Mrs. Cass, who called the Animal Protection Agency when she saw Sassie's transformation from collie to poodle.)

When Winnie was five, she decided to give her dad's fishing worms to Mrs. Cass, who loved her garden. Winnie had heard on TV that worms were a garden's friend. The worms were hearty night crawlers, some a foot and a half long. Winnie had helped her dad harvest them at night with flashlights on the golf course. Her mom wasn't happy Dad kept them in the refrigerator in cottage cheese containers, their long skinny bodies wound around each other like so much dirty spaghetti.

I think Winnie's friendship idea might have worked if she had labeled them worms instead of gift-wrapping them. Also, leaving the package in the ninety-degree heat for the afternoon on Mrs. Cass's porch was not in the worms' long-term interest—or Mrs. Cass's. When she filed the trespassing complaint with the authorities, Mrs. Cass was still shades of moss green edged in purple.

At six and a half Winnie had to be extricated from the chimney when she tried to prove to Jimmy Oates that Santa "could too slide down into the fireplace." Winnie spit soot for a week. As did I. Oh, the depth we angels go to.

At eight years old, Winnie had to be plucked from a telephone pole by the telephone company, which had to send a cherry picker out to rescue her. She had climbed up to see if she could hear voices through the lines. Winnie's big mistake was looking down once she was up. The rescue worker had trouble convincing Winnie it was safe to let go after she had Velcroed herself to the pole. Her mom picked splinters out of Winnie's arms for days. My splinters weren't that easy to reach since I had sat atop the pole to cheer-lead my little climber until help arrived. Oh, the heights we angels go to.

At twelve, Winnie was pretending to drive her mom's van. All might have worked out well had Mrs. Cass not passed by in her BMW at the exact

PATSY CLAIRMONT

moment Winnie shifted the car into reverse and coasted down the driveway. The damage to the neighbor's car exceeded the van's value. Winnie's mom was horn-honking hot.

And so went Winnifred's plans—from catastrophes to disasters to cataclysmic happenings. Oh, the breadth we angels go to. Winnie's mom considered having a Richter scale surgically implanted in her daughter so that the family might have a fighting chance.

Then, at least, when fifteen-year-old Winnie, in a fit of freedom, set the zoo's chimpanzees loose, the family could have detected the seismic movement and hightailed it up to the cabin till the community stopped shaking. Which, by the way, took some time since one of the escapees swung from a tree and dropped smack-dab on top of the police chief's head, knocking off his hairpiece. Winnie's case wasn't helped any by the reporter who snapped a shot of the monkey as he donned the chief's toupee and stuck out his tongue. That pic ran on the front page with the headline, "Chief Flips His Wig While Monkeying Around." Winnie's court plea was temporary insanity while under the influence of a Jane Goodall film.

College didn't prove to be any safer an environment for Winnie, as she made the dean's list within the first semester. No, not the list for academic excellence, the other list. You know, the one for possible expulsion. Seems the darling of the campus was majoring in protests.

That is, until Winnie met my Boss. Whew, I can't begin to tell you how that took pressure off me, her guardian and all. Oh, don't get me wrong; she still is a case, but at least now she will consider my nudges. Like when she met Bill...

Winnie had dated a number of—hmm, how shall I say it—B boys. Borderline losers. Trust me on this; I heard from their guardians firsthand. Then she met Bill at the library. Winnie wasn't impressed, but I was. I started nudging hard. She was standoffish, but gradually, between Bill's sweet disposition and my pointy elbow, Winnie began to see more clearly.

For, as Winnie fell in love with Jesus, her values began to change. But here's the great news: She retained her sense of adventure. In fact, it was enhanced. I'm not sure Bill knew what he was in for, although his wedding day served as a possible primer.

Winnie wanted to surprise Bill at their wedding, which was held in the park across the street from her parents' home. Her plan was to drive up to the altar in a red Corvette convertible that she had rented for their honeymoon trip. (I told you she was colorful.) To add to the festivities, she hired a violinist to stand in the backseat and play "Love Is a Many Splendored Thing" while Winnie eased the 'Vette into the nuptial setting. Winnie had hired Jimmy Oates to release sixteen white doves when the violinist began to play.

Her plan needed to be adapted when she realized she could only drive as close to the altar as the food tables. So she decided that once she parked the car, she could do the traditional hesitation step the rest of the way to the altar. What a laugh. Winnie has never hesitated. No, she definitely was the sort to cartwheel her way to the altar.

The day of their wedding was misty, but that didn't dampen Winnie's spirits. She was aglow. All the invitees took their places, and the service began with a duet singing "All I Ask of You." Then the pastor invited the congregation to stand for the bride, which they did. In the distance the violin's sweet melody could be heard. As the music drew closer, the congregation craned around, trying to determine where it was coming from and where the bride was. This is when things become a little fuzzy as to what happened next.

From friends I have in high places, I've been told that, when Jimmy released the birds, they flew directly over the car, which was the plan. Unfortunately the tension of takeoff was too much for a few of the birds, who released their stress on the violinist, who understandably let out a yelp. But because the yelp sounded like "help," the bride hit the brakes a tad too firmly. The momentum of the stop catapulted the musician onto the bride's head. As Winnie attempted to push the violinist into the backseat, she accidentally hit the gas pedal, which accelerated them through the cake table where they came to a jolting stop inches away from the punch bowl. All three layers of the wedding cake were wrapped around the windshield, with the exception of the bride-and-groom cake topper. It was flipped into the air and landed in the punch bowl where the couple drowned.

The stunned silence that immediately followed this smashing entrance was interrupted by a torrential downpour as the heavens parted. May I just say that Bill was surprised. And he wasn't the only one. Take me, for instance. I was seated on the hood during this falderal. Do you know how difficult it is to remove red punch stains from white wings? (By the way, a special thank-you to Mrs. Cass for calling the police because Winnie drove on the grass. A nice wedding-day touch, neighbor.)

The service was completed—at Winnie's mother's insistence—in Winnie's parents' home where the guests ate ice cream sandwiches Bill bought from the Good Humor Man, who was driving by. People in Sourgum, Virginia, still speak of that wedding.

Today Bill and Winnie have four children. (This pleases her mom, who hopes they are all like Winnie.) Winnie, wanting to be active in the direction local education takes for her family, has decided being part of the PTA is the "sensible" way to do it. Yet she realizes having her life audited may open her to a tough process to boogie her way through. And even though she keeps reminding herself that God mercifully measures each of us, who among us would want to volunteer for close scrutiny of our lives knowing that the one who holds the final vote is Mrs. Cass?

THE WEDDING RING

On a blustery fall day Dilly Thornton stood in the Ohio cemetery staring at a gray headstone. Leaves from a maple fluttered to the ground and encircled her feet like an autumn wreath. As a chilling gust of wind caused her to seek refuge deeper in her dark trench coat, she gathered the strength to remember how she had ended up in this place.

For forty-two years Dilly had walked at Hank's side, and now he was gone. Cause of death was listed as a heart attack, but she knew in actuality his heart finally had turned to stone. She had married him when she was only nineteen, a carefree, pretty girl, and he a handsome, thirty-one-year-old farmer. She naively had mistaken his controlling personality as levelheaded decisiveness, and what she thought was his purposeful ways was actually directed anger, which after their wedding was directed at her.

In the beginning of their marriage Dilly was confused by Hank's sullenness, followed by his intimidating outbursts of anger. Eventually his possessiveness led to the erosion of all her important relationships until she found herself in a relational desert. He didn't want children interfering in his life so she laid that dream to rest early in their marriage; later she thought it wisdom.

For more than two decades Dilly believed that, if she just tried harder to be the kind of woman Hank thought she should be, he would become less volatile and more content. But as the years dissolved, so did her hope that her existence would ever be happy or that he would ever be at peace with her. He made sure he snuffed out any embers of joy.

Now Dilly traced Hank's chiseled name in the cold stone and remembered her conversation with the funeral director when she ordered it.

"Mrs. Thornton, we have some beautiful headstones for husbands and wives. The stone will bear both your names, and we will leave the date of your death open."

"No," Dilly answered in a low, steady voice, "I do not want my name on the same stone as his."

The director leaned in as if wondering if he had heard correctly. Dilly noted how the line between his eyebrows had deepened under the strain of comprehending her meaning. Then he inquired, "Do you mean you would like separate stones?"

Dilly looked up at the director. "Sir, I don't even want to be buried in the same cemetery as Hank. I was forced to lie alongside him in life, but I refuse to lie near him in death."

And so it was. Now Hank had his own gravestone, and Dilly was standing next to the fresh mound of dirt. Devoid of feelings, she announced to the wind, "Forgive me for not crying, but I've shed my tears for over forty years. I don't have any left." Then she pulled her driving gloves from her coat pocket and stretched them over her work-worn hands. After hesitating a moment she pulled off her left-hand glove, removed her wedding band, knelt down, and pressed it deep into the loose soil near the gravestone. Then she walked away without looking back.

Dilly awoke the next morning to sunlight as it dusted the edge of her bed in warmth. She felt a weight on her heart, and then she remembered Hank was gone. The weight lifted and was replaced with an almost giddy feeling. For decades she had made her daily decisions through Hank's grid, but no more. His iron hand had turned to dust.

Dilly slipped into her robe and slippers and then headed down to the kitchen. As she descended the staircase, she laughed aloud at the sheer outrageousness of her behavior. For, in all the years of her marriage, even if she was ill, she wasn't allowed to come to the kitchen table unless she was dressed for the day. Hank insisted that decent women did not parade about in nightclothes. But this day, for her own enjoyment, Dilly marched back and forth several times in the kitchen with her hair askew as she sang "I Love a Parade." Then she sat down at the table, put her head in her hands, and cried.

"Oh, Lord, I'm a mess. I can't decide what to feel. I know Hank was my husband, and while I'm not glad he died, on many levels it's a relief. His stringent ways and his cruel heart have left me emotionally undone. I'm uncertain of what to do now that the gate of my life has been thrown open so wide. I feel like a child who has gone from her wading pool to the ocean's edge: thrilled yet threatened. Please take my hand; don't let me drown."

Then Dilly wandered about her home and tried to decide what to do next. She dressed and began to pack up some of Hank's belongings. After putting his clothes into some garbage bags she intended to send to Goodwill, she boxed up his personal items and placed them on a shelf in the closet. When she finished, she lay across her bed and wept tears she was surprised she had, until she fell asleep from exhaustion.

Dilly was startled awake by the telephone. "Hello," she answered groggily.

"Mrs. Thornton?" a voice asked.

"Yes. Who is this?"

"My name is Pastor Toomey from Grace Chapel. One of your neighbors brought to my attention that your husband died recently. I just wanted to extend my sympathy and ask if our church might be of help to you during this difficult time?"

"Thank you. I can't think of anything, but I appreciate the offer." The kind words made Dilly feel a little weepy.

"Would you mind if a couple of the ladies from the church dropped by to meet you?"

Dilly wasn't sure she was ready to have strangers in her home. Yet she longed for someone to talk to. Hank would never have allowed church folks to come over, but he couldn't stop her now. Unsure of how she felt, Dilly heard herself respond, "That would be pleasant. Thank you."

"Would tomorrow afternoon around two o'clock be good for you?"

"That would be fine." Dilly hung up and wondered if her decision was wise. Hank always told her that church ladies were just busybodies butting in where they didn't belong, but then Hank didn't have room in his heart for anyone.

The next afternoon Dilly watched as two women approached her door. Both looked to be in their midthirties. One woman wore her dark hair pulled back in a bun that accented her face's lovely bone structure. The other, a blonde, was a bit "chunky," as Hank would have said.

For a moment Dilly considered hiding. Then, mustering her courage, she opened the door.

"Hello, Mrs. Thornton, we're from Grace Chapel," the woman with the bun said. "My name is Sandra Choi, and this is Amy Miller."

"Please come in. I've been expecting you." Dilly toyed with confessing that she almost had called the pastor to tell them not to come, but she decided that wouldn't be polite. "May I fix you a cup of tea?" she said instead.

"If you would heat some water, we've brought cups and tea bags for the three of us." Amy pulled cups and napkins out of a basket she had carried in.

Dilly put on the kettle and came back to the living room where the two women had set up a small tea party, complete with scones. Dilly was impressed at how easy these ladies were making this visit for her.

After their tea was steeping in the cups, Dilly's guests turned the conversation from the weather outside to the storm inside her life.

"Mrs. Thornton, we know this is a difficult time, and we don't want to add to your pain, but we would like to be a listening ear, if that would help," Sandra offered.

"That's very thoughtful. I really don't have anyone to talk to. Hank and I didn't have children, and we were both from small families. My parents are deceased, and I was an only child." Dilly sat quietly, pondering the truth of what she had just said. Then she stirred herself to go on. "Hank and I were married for over forty years. He always worked the land; he loved being a farmer. Not an easy life, but he made a good living for us. He had a massive heart attack while sitting on the tractor. One of our hired hands found him slumped over the wheel. So he died doing what he loved. I guess we all hope for that."

"Will you stay on in this charming farmhouse?" Amy asked.

"I don't know. It's so cumbersome for one body. It seems like there are rooms at every turn, full of the loudest silence I've ever heard. But thank you for saying it's charming. I guess I've never thought of it in that way." Dilly looked around at the plain furnishings she had been forced to endure because Hank said they were good enough. Her parents had left her some lovely antiques, but they were stored because Hank wouldn't allow her to bring them into his house. A fresh pang of resentment stabbed at her heart.

"I'm thinking of redecorating," she announced to herself as well as to her guests. "I have some old family pieces in the storage building out back that I think will look good in here."

"Perhaps I could be of some help with that, Mrs. Thornton," Sandra suggested. "I have a strong back and a pretty good decorating eye, if you need some assistance."

"Me, too. Well, at least I have a strong back," Amy confessed with a smile.

"How sweet of you both. Thank you."

"We mean it. Please let us be a part," Amy urged.

Dilly studied them and saw how sincere their offer was. "You both have been so kind to listen to me ramble, and yes, I'd be grateful for your help."

The visitors parted after agreeing to return on the weekend. Dilly was pleased with the conversation because they hadn't lingered on Hank. She didn't want to expose her own misery, nor did she want to smudge his character. She felt Hank had done a good enough job of that without her help. She just wanted to get on with her life.

In the following days, that's exactly what Dilly tried to do. But she felt as if she were in a maze because so many new twists and turns greeted her, each demanding choices—always more choices.

Then, one day as she was contemplating where she would place various pieces of her parents' furniture, she heard, "Mrs. Thornton. Mrs. Thornton." Dwayne, one of the hired men, was calling from the front door.

Dilly opened her upstairs window. "Yes, Dwayne?"

"Did you want Bob and me to finish turning over the back field that we started before Mr. Thornton left us?" Dwayne pulled off his hat and curled the brim.

Dilly wasn't sure what they should be doing, but she believed Dwayne was a good man and could be trusted. "What do you think, Dwayne? Is that where we should be placing our efforts today?"

"Yes ma'am, that and getting the repairs done on the barn."

"Okay, Dwayne. That will be fine."

Afterwards Dilly thought, *I need to sell this place. I don't know how to run a farm.* Then she caught herself and said aloud, "Wait. I've lived and worked on this farm for years. If anyone should know how to run it, I ought to." With that admission she grabbed a pencil and paper and wrote down a list of things that would need to be done over the next few months, and then she prioritized them. When she finished, she posted them on the front of her refrigerator and made up her mind to meet with Dwayne.

But the next morning her resolve to manage the farm began to waver. Hank had told her that she had sawdust for brains, and she was beginning to believe him. Then again, maybe she always had believed him.

"Mrs. Thornton. Mrs. Thornton."

Dilly wondered why Dwayne always stood outside and called her instead of ringing the doorbell. She opened the door, and the faithful worker stood with his hat in his hand, nervously working the brim. "Hello, Dwayne. Why don't you join me for a few minutes to discuss the chores."

"Sure, ma'am. Be glad to," he replied, looking almost embarrassed.

Dilly showed Dwayne her list, and he seemed impressed and relieved to see she had a plan. "Dwayne, would you be my foreman until I decide if I'm staying on?"

"Foreman?" He looked amazed.

"How long have you been with us?"

"Ten years next fall, Miz Thornton," he announced proudly.

"I'll only say this once about my husband, and then I won't speak of it again. That's the longest any hired hand has lasted with Hank. He wasn't an easy man to work for."

"No ma'am. He sure wasn't," Dwayne spoke almost in a whisper.

"You've been a faithful worker and endured a powerful taskmaster. Thank you for your years of service. I hope you'll stay on and help me out."

"I'd be proud to, Miz Thornton." Dwayne stood to leave.

"One thing I'd ask different of you from now on, Dwayne. Would you please ring the doorbell when you need me instead of yelling?"

"Yes ma'am." He grinned and looked down at his boots.

"Dwayne, I'll make sure you are well compensated for your added responsibility."

Once at the door, Dwayne turned back and tipped the brim of his hat. "I don't want to speak out of place, ma'am, but I'd just like to say that nobody's been more faithful than you. You are a strong woman. It's a privilege to work for you." Then he walked away.

Me? A strong woman? Me, who couldn't choose this morning between an egg or oatmeal? Me, who has sawdust for brains? Dilly sat down and had a good cry. When she stood up, she felt as if something inside of her wasn't quite so wobbly.

The weekend arrived, and with it a beautiful Indian summer day, and Sandra and Amy returned as promised. The three women toted some of the furniture in a wheelbarrow and some on a wagon hooked to the back of a tractor. They handled everything except the large black walnut dining room table that Dwayne and a worker brought into the house for them. For three hours Sandra and Amy helped Dilly scoot, push, and pull the furniture around until everything had a place.

Falling into chairs around the living room, they looked at their efforts with pleasure. "Hey, we're good," Sandra said with a laugh.

"Yeah, but look at us now." Amy indicated their limp postures and pooped expressions.

"I wouldn't want to do this for a living," Dilly giggled, wiping her brow.

Sandra looked at Dilly and said, "I think you're going to enjoy this. It really looks lovely."

"And homey," Amy added.

Dilly leaned back and tried to take it all in. The rooms were transformed by the rich woods and beautiful fabrics of the furnishings. The house had turned out more beautiful than she could have imagined.

Suddenly, without warning, tears again flooded Dilly's face. Embarrassed, she excused herself and headed for the privacy of the bathroom. Finally, after pulling herself together, she walked back into the living room, only to find Sandra and Amy gone. Afraid she had made them uncomfortable with her emotional outburst, she went to the door to see if they had driven away. Instead, she found them pulling a picnic out of the trunk of their car. Relieved they hadn't left, she joined them under one of the large oaks in the front yard where the women ate and visited.

That evening Dilly mentally assessed her day and was pleased. She thought how fortunate she was to have had Amy and Sandra's help. During their picnic Dilly had learned that Amy was a substitute teacher and Sandra was a caseworker for the Toledo Child Protection Division.

Sandra had shared some sad stories about the neglected and abused children she encountered, and the stories touched Dilly's heart. She admired Sandra's investment in the lives of others. Then Dilly realized she had spent most of her energies surviving her trying marriage.

"Lord, I want my life to count, but most of my years are behind me. Is there some way I could make up for all those lost years? Or at least use the time I have left in significant ways? Lead me, Lord, and help me to be wise enough to follow."

Sandra began to pick up Dilly on Sunday mornings for church. Afterwards Sandra and Amy, when she could, would join Dilly for lunch at the farm. The women helped Dilly can green beans and paint her kitchen. The three even started a kitchen outreach in which they would cook up food baskets at Dilly's, and then Amy and Sandra would deliver them to people in the community. As the weeks turned into months, Dilly grew fond of these two women who had added so much joy to her existence.

Then one day Amy surprised Dilly and Sandra by announcing she was being transferred to another school district where she could teach full time. They all celebrated her good fortune, for it was an answer to their joint prayers, even though Dilly and Sandra would miss Amy's sweet ways.

Shortly after that, as Sandra and Dilly drove to church, Dilly noticed Sandra was distracted and troubled. Her usual upbeat ways seemed smothered by a thick cloud of melancholy.

"Sandra, you seem down today. Is something wrong?"

"Oh, I'm sorry. I didn't mean for it to be so obvious. I've been dealing with a little girl, Patty Matthews, and things aren't working out well. I was hoping her mom would respond to our offers of help, but finally I had to have Patty removed from her home to protect her. It breaks my heart." Tears welled up in Sandra's brown eyes.

"You really care for this child, don't you?" Dilly asked, as she reached in her pocket for a handkerchief to give to Sandra.

"Yes, I do. My family's so far away. With my parents in China as missionaries for four more years before I see them again, I want some kind of family here. Someone to love and to come home to. Perhaps it's my biological clock ticking, but I want to be Patty's mom. I was trained not to get this emotionally involved with the families because there's no end to the needs of people and we personally can't take them all on, but I really love this neglected child." Sandra wiped her eyes with Dilly's hankie.

"Where is Patty now?"

"I have her in a temporary foster home while I look for a more permanent place."

"Why don't you take her?"

"Don't think I haven't considered it. But my work hours are so erratic, and Patty needs special attention. She has some learning struggles and mood swings that require someone to work closely with her. I want to be that someone, Dilly. I just don't know how I can arrange it."

"Didn't you tell me once that all things are possible with God?" Dilly patted her friend's hand.

"Yes, but I'm afraid it's easier to believe that for someone else than for myself."

"How true, how true." Dilly thought for a moment and then said, "Listen, Sandra, after the service today, why don't we pick up Patty and take her out to the farm? We could have a picnic and go for a good old country stroll. She'd probably enjoy seeing our horses, the milk cow, and even Mellow, that big yellow barn cat, if we can find her."

Sandra's eyes sparkled. "That's a great idea. You go in and save me a seat. I'll call ahead to make arrangements with Patty's foster mom." Sandra let Dilly out in front of the church and went in search of a parking place.

When Sandra slid into the pew, she smiled at Dilly to indicate the plan was set. Dilly felt good that she had thought of at least a small way to give back to Sandra, who had been so thoughtful and helpful to her over the past few months. It wasn't a full solution, but for today the smile was back on Sandra's face.

The pastor's message, about Peter walking to Jesus on the water, was entitled, "Taking the Next Shaky Step." Dilly noticed that Sandra seemed to be listening almost as carefully as she was herself.

That afternoon Dilly understood why Sandra was so fond of Patty. The chubby little seven-year-old had a short crop of curly blond hair that seemed to twist around in all directions, as if unsure of which way to go. And she had the most endearing crooked little smile. But the child's heart was what captured Dilly's attention as she watched the youngster repeatedly try, with her handicapped leg, to ride the old bicycle from the barn.

Dwayne came by, saw Patty's dilemma, and jury-rigged the pedal to accommodate her disability. Dilly and Sandra applauded and cheered as Patty managed her first solo ride.

As the weeks went by, the trio found they made a good team in whatever they did: crafts, games, or even wallpapering.

Then one afternoon, when Dilly was reading to Patty, she noticed that Patty was carefully studying Dilly's face. "What is it, Patty? Is something wrong?"

"No," the child answered, "I just wondered how old you are."

Dilly, amused, asked, "And why were you wondering?"

"'Cause I wondered if you were old enough to be a grandmother."

"Yes, I'm certainly old enough." Dilly chuckled.

"Well, I've always wanted one of those," Patty said.

"Well, Patty, I've always wanted a granddaughter. Do you think we could make a deal? How about if you call me 'Grandma,' and I'll call you my granddaughter? Would that work?"

Patty's crooked smile spread across her face like a rainbow. "Grandma Dilly," she said, as if practicing the name.

"Yes, Granddaughter," Dilly answered.

Patty grinned again.

Several weeks later Patty asked, "Grandma Dilly, why are your eyes so sad? Did your mommy and daddy leave you, too?"

Dilly's breath caught in her throat. She ached for this child, who had been so easily discarded and whose insights far exceeded her years. "Patty, everybody has some sadness."

"Is that why Sandra cries when she takes me back to the foster home—'cause she's sad?"

"Mmm, I suppose. And because she loves you."

"Do you love me, Grandma Dilly?" Patty tilted her head to one side as she watched Dilly.

Dilly was impressed that Patty would risk such a question. "Yes I do, Patty."

"Then if I hug you, will that make your eyes happy?"

"It will certainly help."

Patty wrapped her chubby arms around Dilly. Dilly's eyes began to drip.

"These are happy tears, Patty. Thank you for that hug. I can tell already it's helping."

That evening Dilly knelt next to her bed in a pool of moonlight. "Lord, today when Patty hugged me, I realized that in spite of the cruelty she has had to bear, she has somehow remained innocent, which is in stark contrast to the bitterness and resentment I carry in my heart. Patty reaches out and loves others. I know for me to do the same, I need to be a Peter and take the next shaky step. So here goes…Lord, forgive me, a sinner, for passing judgment on my fractured husband. I was an adult; I could have made other choices. Forgive me for blaming him all these years for my joyless existence. You are the Joy Giver—not my circumstances, not my mate, but You, Lord. Release me from the cords that keep me bound to Hank's hostility. Grant me the inner liberty to rise up and live and love for You. Amen."

That night Dilly slept deeply and well. When she awoke the next day, it was with a clean heart and a clear plan. The first thing she did was call the Child Protection Division and ask for Sandra.

"Hello, Sandra Choi."

"Sandra, this is Dilly. I'd like to fill out forms to become a foster parent."

"Huh? A foster parent? You're kidding, right?"

"Kidding? Of course not. I want Patty to live with me."

"You would take Patty?" Dilly heard the tears in Sandra's voice.

"I thought you'd be happy."

"Happy? I'm elated!"

"Sandra, there's one condition, though."

"Name it."

"I want you to live with us, too. Patty and I need you in our lives. Let us be your family to come home to. You can be Patty's foster mom, and I'll be her foster grandmother…Sandra? Hello? Sandra?"

"I'm here," Sandra responded in a little voice.

"Well, for heaven's sake say something. Say yes. You know I have the room, and think of all the ways the three of us could fill them with joy."

"This is one of the best days of my life. Thank you, Dilly, thank you!"

"Is that a yes?"

"Yes! Yes! Yes!…Dilly, I've never been a mom. Will you help me?"

"Sandra, I've never been a grandma. We'll help each other."

"Will you go with me to tell Patty?"

"I will, if you don't mind swinging by the cemetery. I need to pick up something I left there."

GRANDMA MOSES

School was out for the summer, and no one was more relieved than eleven-year-old Sarah Lynn Wade. Not that she didn't like school—she was a B-plus student—but year-end monotony had set in, and she was ready for some late mornings and unstructured days. Sarah understood her family couldn't venture off for a vacation, like many of her friends, because money was tight and her dad's hours at work had been cut. But no vacation was just fine since she had her own plans. She was going to join forces with Grandma Moses.

Mind you, Grandma Moses wasn't Sarah's grandma, and her name wasn't Moses. The neighbors gave her that title because they claimed she was always trying to lead people to the Promised Land. Sarah lived five houses away from Grandma Moses and her famous garden where she raised vegetables for the poor families in neighboring communities. Grandma was even featured in a senior citizens' magazine. She claimed they spotlighted her because she was a Golden Oldie; she was eighty-five. It sometimes slipped people's minds, though, because, despite her wrinkles and all, she just seemed downright, well, youthful.

Sarah loved helping Grandma Moses work in the garden with its array of flowers and vegetables. That's what Sarah had done last summer, and this year during spring break she had seeded the beds with Grandma. Now the time had come to concentrate on the garden once again.

But Sarah was surprised to learn, on the first day of vacation, that she wasn't the only one who had a plan for her summer. Her dad felt she needed to focus her efforts at home, assisting her mom with additional household chores. In fact, he called a family meeting for the three of them so they would "all be on the same page." When Sarah heard his demands, she felt they weren't even reading the same book.

"Sarah, this summer I don't want you to think you can just flit around the neighborhood without consideration for the needs right here at home," her father stated in somber tones, his bushy eyebrows bunched together from scowling. "I want you to help your mom around the house and help me with the yard. You're growing up, and that means learning to take on more responsibilities. Life isn't easy, Sarah, and you need to be prepared for the difficulties it brings."

With each word her dad spoke, Sarah's delight in the summer that stretched before her further dissipated. Then, after his "Summer Is Now in Session" speech, he handed Sarah a list of chores she was to accomplish that day and informed her he would make such a list for her every day. She began to think she would never get to spend time in Grandma's garden.

Grandma laughed a lot, and Sarah needed some joyful noise. In fact, Grandma was always saying funny things, although her friends weren't sure she knew it. Last summer Sarah remembered a time when Grandma went to pluck some cucumbers for a salad but instead picked up a big fat frog. She let out a shriek of surprise and then doubled over in giggles. When Sarah arrived at that row to see what had happened, Grandma looked up at her and exclaimed, "I almost croaked." Sarah looked at the fat frog and then into Grandma's face, full of fun. Sarah laughed until she cried. Grandma always said laughing was as good for a body as sunshine.

But laughter wasn't on her father's agenda. As a matter of fact, as Sarah dusted the furniture (number seven on the to-do list), her father bellowed, "Sarah Lynn, come here right this minute."

Her stomach knotted as she headed for the kitchen. "Yes, Dad."

"Did I or did I not ask you to put the lid back on the garbage can?"

"I did," Sarah replied, trying not to sound whiny.

"Look out the window, young lady, and tell me what you see." Her dad's voice, loud and heated, sounded to Sarah like the broken muffler on his car.

Just then Sarah's mom came to her rescue. "John, that wasn't Sarah's fault. After she replaced the lid, I backed into the can and dented it, and then the lid wouldn't fit back on."

"How could you back into the can?" He looked stunned.

"It really was quite easy. I thought I had the car in drive, but it was in reverse." Mom winked at both of them over her shoulder and then turned to do the dishes.

Sarah's dad snapped, "Sarah, you'd better finish dusting." Then he buried his face in the newspaper.

Tears stung her eyes as she grabbed some tissues and headed back to the dusting. Eventually she made it through the assignments, and then she marched down the street to Grandma Moses' garden, feeling as though a cloud moved with her.

"Hi, Grandma, I'm here," Sarah mumbled as she headed for the shed to find some work gloves.

"Hello, Wee One. You don't sound very chipper," Grandma answered from the strawberry patch where she was feeding the plants.

"Oh, it's my dad again. I don't think he likes me. He seems to look for reasons to be mad at me."

"Listen, child, your daddy has a lot on his mind. It's not easy to carry the responsibility for a family. Your daddy is like my prize tomatoes; he just needs some support, someone to lean on to help him handle his load. Don't you remember how last summer, before we staked those tomatoes, the weight of them was snapping the vines? Then we propped them up, and they did splendidly. Won us a first place ribbon at the state fair, by Job."

Grandma was quiet for a moment and then said, "Sarah, you weed in the tomato patch today for me, would you, dear?"

Sarah didn't think the tomatoes needed weeding, but she did it anyway. As she worked, she noted how the big red fruit hung from the vines like brilliant rubies gleaming from the treasure chest of a king. She agreed with Grandma that the propped-up tomatoes were splendid.

"Grandma," Sarah called over the vines, "how can I prop up my dad?"

"Prayer, honey, prayer. You pray for your dad to grow strong in the Lord, and God will help hold him up."

Grandma talked to God a lot. She talked to herself a lot too. She said she was praying, but one time Sarah heard her complaining about her phone bill to the turnips. Sarah didn't mind. Sometimes she talked to her rag doll when no one was around. Sarah figured she was old enough to be done with dolls, but at times she found it comforting to talk to someone who would never tell what she had said. Mostly she told her doll things about her dad when he hurt her feelings.

Grandma said people were like garden produce. If that was true, then Sarah figured her dad was an onion because he made her cry.

When Sarah finished with the tomato weeding, she asked Grandma, "Would you pray for my dad?"

"I think we'd better pray for him together. You see, Sarah, two people praying is twice the support."

"But I don't know how to pray out loud, Grandma."

"Oh, child, it's just like praying by yourself, only louder."

Grandma always made hard things simple. The two of them prayed, and Sarah felt better. Even though her daddy still seemed cranky when she went home that night, she just kept thinking about those tomatoes.

The next day Sarah headed for Grandma Moses' as soon as her list of chores was complete, which meant it was well into the afternoon. Her job for the day, Grandma explained, was to deadhead the petunias.

Sarah especially enjoyed the flowers in the garden. Dahlias were her favorite. She used to like the peonies best, but one day she bent down to smell one and sniffed an ant right into her nose. It tickled so that she sneezed that ant right into the bleeding hearts. Now she liked dahlias.

While Sarah worked, Grandma did, too, leaning her slender frame on a staff to steady herself as she rose up and down among the plants. Watching her bob around the half-acre reminded Sarah of a scarecrow who couldn't decide where to stand. Grandma wore a bandanna handkerchief tied around her head with a straw hat over it to shade her crinkled face and her warm gray eyes. Her yellow garden clogs peeked out beneath the generous overalls that seemed to swallow her.

"Let's take a break," Grandma invited Sarah after they had worked in happy silence for a while.

Grandma pulled up a couple of carrots and rinsed them under the spigot on the side of her house. The two gardeners sat in the shade of a nearby maple tree and ate the sweet and crunchy snacks.

"Tomorrow we'll harvest some carrots," Grandma announced.

So the next day they pulled two bushel baskets of carrots and dug up two bushels of potatoes. Later the Salvation Army truck would pick them up and give them to families that didn't get many fresh vegetables. Grandma always said, "Givin' is livin'."

But gardening didn't always go easily. With August came two weeks of no rain, and they had to carry water to parts of the garden. Filling buckets at the spigot, they then placed the buckets in wagons, and pulled the wagons through the rows to the plants that the sprinklers didn't reach. The work was hot and hard.

Then one day while Grandma was tending her tomatoes and Sarah was cutting some droopy black-eyed Susans, a rain shower began, ending the drought. Grandma and Sarah met at the rutabagas and danced in the rain. Then they headed for the porch's shelter arm in arm, laughing.

"Thanks for dancing before the Lord with me, Sarah," Grandma said as she wiped the rain from her face.

"I didn't know that was what we were doing," Sarah said, "but I liked it."

Once the rain stopped, the two trooped back to the garden.

"Grandma, what's your real name?" Sarah inquired.

Grandma announced proudly, "Mabel Slotman."

"Mabel?" Sarah repeated, scrunching up her nose. "Mabel Slotman?"

"But you, Sarah, may call me Moses."

Both of them giggled.

"One day," Grandma explained, "we'll have new names in heaven. I hope mine will be 'Faithful One.'"

Sarah thought about a new name for days. Finally she decided she would like hers to be "Dahlia."

Several days passed, and Sarah's lists of chores were longer than usual. She completed all the tasks set before her, but her mind was full of pictures of a certain garden that needed lots of tending and Grandma Moses working alone in the hot sun.

Finally a day came when the list was shorter, and Sarah dashed over to the garden just after lunch. But on her way she saw Twila, a neighborhood girl her age, walking down the street. She was munching on a DoveBar she must have bought from the ice cream truck. Sarah could hear its jingling songs a block or so down the street.

"Hi, Sarah," Twila said, pausing to chat as she licked the chocolate bar.

"Hi, Twila. Um, I have to hurry; Grandma Moses is expecting me." Sarah kept on moving, eager to see Grandma and eager to avoid Twila.

"Okay," Twila said with a shrug of her shoulders.

Sarah shrugged her own shoulders and hurried over to the picket fence that marked Grandma's yard.

Grandma was putting empty milk jugs on wooden stakes to scare any rabbits that might meander into the garden and suggested Sarah help. While they worked, Sarah mentioned she didn't like Twila.

"Why, Sarah?" Grandma asked, her eyes searching Sarah's.

"Oh, she brags too much. You know, like about her straight A's and stuff." Sarah avoided Grandma's gaze.

"Wee One, bad thoughts about folks are like weeds. Left unattended they will take over the garden and choke the life out of it."

Then wouldn't you know it, Grandma switched Sarah's duty to weed control for the rest of the week. Probably so Sarah would get the point. Sarah figured she should never have told Grandma.

The following Tuesday, Sarah walked down to the garden in the morning and who was helping Grandma bring in the cucumbers? Yep, it was Twila.

What if Grandma wanted a more consistent helper? Sarah thought. What if her dad had caused her to lose her gardener's position? Sarah felt anger burn toward her father.

"Sarah," Grandma called, "hurry, child. We need your help; the truck will be here soon. You assist Twila while I find more baskets."

Not left with much choice, Sarah handed up the cukes to Twila, who nestled them in baskets. Turned out Twila was kind of fun. The team effort and one previous week's work in the garden helped to weed out Sarah's thoughts about Twila.

After the truck picked up the produce, Grandma invited both girls to join her for a cup of tea on the front porch. She had each girl select a cup from the hutch in her kitchen. Sarah chose one with a single rose on the outside and a pink petal on the inside. Twila picked a cup with lilies of the valley painted all the way around it.

The tea was made with the peppermint that grew under Grandma's spigot. It smelled so good steaming up into their faces, and they sweetened the tea with some gooey honey from a comb. Grandma placed a dish of shortbread cookies in front of the girls and then announced she had to make a phone call and would be back soon. By the time she joined them again, Twila and Sarah had eaten most of the cookies and had made afternoon plans to play putt-putt golf.

On Saturday morning, after Sarah made her bed and washed the breakfast dishes, she headed for Grandma's. Sarah had promised her she would string twine to the fence post for the sweet peas to trail on.

But when Sarah arrived, Grandma wasn't in sight, so Sarah headed for the potting shed to find the twine. What she found instead was Grandma. She was sitting on the floor with a burlap bag thrown over her legs. She looked up at Sarah and smiled weakly.

"Sarah, honey, would you please run down and ask your mom to come here for a minute?"

Even though Grandma was calm, somehow Sarah knew she was in trouble and Sarah ran like the wind. Her heart was pounding by the time she dashed in the house yelling, "Mom, come quick! Grandma's on the floor of the shed. I think she's hurt!"

Sarah's mom hurried back with her, and Grandma told her she had twisted her ankle when she fell over a rake handle and just needed a little help to get up and into the house. Instead, Sarah's mom took her to the emergency clinic. Grandma had a mild sprain. Of course, that meant she had to use a cane for a while.

For the rest of the summer, Sarah and Twila became Grandma Moses' right and left hands. She called them her Aaron and Miriam. Grandma would sit in a chair at the end of a row and tell them what she wanted done. Sarah's mom came down several times over the next two weeks and helped work the garden.

Then, one Wednesday evening, as they harvested lettuce and radishes, Sarah saw some movement by the picket fence and stopped long enough to glance up. Her father was walking toward them.

Sarah thought, *Now what did I do?* But her father was smiling—something he had started doing since he found out that he was to receive a pay raise and work more hours.

"Evening, Grandma Moses," he said, as if he showed up in the garden every day.

"Evening, Henry," Grandma Moses said.

"I thought I'd come over to mow your grass and to load the baskets of food into the delivery truck."

"That would be really nice," Grandma said, shooting Sarah a smile with her eyes as if to say, "Your dad is one fine tomato."

Once Grandma was back on her feet she decided to have a year-end neighborhood garden party to celebrate "God's bountiful blessings." The next few days were busy as Grandma, Sarah, and Twila planned, pruned, and patched the garden and yard. And Sarah's parents announced they would help. Her dad fixed the fences near the rutabagas and the pumpkins, where they had needed mending for some time. Sarah and her mom whitewashed the fence to clean it up. Twila and her mom sewed pictures of fruits and vegetables to make garden flags. And once the fence post paint was dry, they tied the flags onto them. Grandma didn't seem to realize it, but every time she passed the flags she would hum "His Banner Over Me Is Love."

The day of the celebration, Sarah's mom fixed corn on the cob with skewer handles, and Twila's mom cut up fruit and served it in watermelon boats. Grandma and Sarah made a huge vegetable salad that was served out of a wheelbarrow that had been scrubbed and lined with a new shower curtain and a checkered tablecloth. Twila and her dad grilled chicken legs, and Sarah's dad made homemade peach ice cream that was scooped into small Mason jars for bowls.

Sarah took her dad by the arm and led him down the row to see the prize tomatoes. He must have liked them a lot because he hugged her and said, "Sarah, you've done a good job."

Grandma made a speech after dinner. She rang an old rusty dinner bell until all the chatter stopped. "I want to thank all of you for being so kind to me since my fall. Thank you, Beth, for taking me for medical attention, for helping in the garden, and for allowing Sarah to work with me."

Next Grandma pointed to Sarah's dad. "Thank you, Henry, for mowing my grass and mending my fences these past few weeks."

Then Grandma walked right up to Sarah's dad and gave him a hug in front of everyone. And he hugged her back. It was a long hug. Sarah couldn't decide who was holding up whom. They both seemed to be in need of support like those tomatoes Grandma bragged on. Then Grandma hugged Sarah's mom, Twila's mom and dad, and, finally, she called Sarah and Twila to her side.

"I want you all to know that these young ladies have been handmaidens of the Lord sent to bless me so that I might continue to feed others."

Everyone applauded. Twila and Sarah giggled and turned radish red.

"The Lord is the giver of all good gifts," Grandma announced, "and I would like you to join me in a prayer of thanksgiving. Please hold hands and bow your heads as I pray."

When the prayer ended Sarah looked up at her dad. His eyes looked watery, and his face seemed softer.

As they walked home, he held Sarah's hand.

School started the next day, so for the time being, Sarah's garden days were limited. But she thought about the garden a lot and how people were like fruits, vegetables, and flowers. And she decided she didn't want her new name to be Dahlia. The week before, when she had knelt down to admire her future namesake, a bee had stung her. No, forget Dahlia. Sarah would rather her new name be Mabel.

CHRISTMAS CABIN

*J*ulya Lennon felt she was living inside a Christmas card as she prepared goodies for the evening's festivities. While she shredded angel food cake to layer in a torte, strains of "Joy to the World" wafted through the kitchen from an old Philco floor radio tucked in the corner. The intermingled fragrances of pine needles, oranges, and cinnamon pleased her senses, as did the sight through the windowpanes of pirouetting snowflakes. Two flickering oil lamps on a buffet sent amber shadows waltzing across the rough-hewn log walls, and a plump Christmas tree waiting to be adorned filled a corner in the living room. Across from the tree the fireplace crackled with just the right warmth and light to make the scene picture perfect.

Spending Christmas in the Colorado mountains was a delayed dream come true for forty-nine-year-old Julya. Her business-minded husband of twenty-five years, Scott, had been in no hurry to deal with the winter precipitation and isolation. He was a city boy and, unlike Julya, found no romance in Douglas firs dappled in fresh mounds of snow or quiet so loud it could be felt. Her husband preferred the Denver nightscape that lit the evening like strings of tree lights while the rhythm of the holiday bustle filled the air. Scott also appreciated the teams of youth who for a reasonable fee would shovel away any snow accumulation that would hinder his progress. Julya saw the snowy mountains as inviting, whereas Scott didn't relish the challenge of digging his way in and out of a remote cabin in the name of celebration.

The six-room log cabin had been in Scott's family for several generations, and after his father's death, it had become Scott's. For years, when their two sons, Robert and Jason, were growing up, they would spend several weeks each summer at the mountain retreat, swimming, fishing, and exploring wooded trails. Always Julya would say longingly before they would leave, "What a glorious place this would be to celebrate Christmas." Somehow Scott was able to dissuade her year after year, his excuses as elaborate as his gifts, in hopes Julya would give up her Currier and Ives dream.

But in April Julya was diagnosed with breast cancer, catapulting the entire family into the trauma of possibly losing her. After she had a radical mastectomy and chemotherapy, the doctor gave her a cautious yet optimistic diagnosis.

Julya had waded through the endless tests and hospitalization with grace and courage, but afterwards she struggled with an inexplicable sadness. One day her husband, sons, and their wives announced to her their decision to have Julya's long awaited holiday in the mountains.

At first Julya was reluctant, finding enthusiasm for anything in life difficult, but gradually she once again embraced her Christmas dream. Scott and Julya arrived in the mountains first, choosing to come up and ready the log hideaway with supplies and decorations. The rest of the family would join them Christmas Eve. On arrival, Scott's sage-colored 4x4 bulged with gifts and groceries, which required multiple trips to the cabin to unload. Julya knew she had packed enough decorations to dress Carnegie Hall elaborately, much less a cabin, but the mental lethargy she was battling made even simple decisions difficult; so she just brought everything.

Once Julya began the holiday preparations around the homey cabin, she felt a little inner buoyancy, as though weights were gradually being lifted from her mind and emotions. She hummed along with the carols in an attempt to support this lighter attitude lest she spiral back down into the bottomless gloom that so easily beset her these days. To Julya the sadness seemed to have settled in one day, much like a swarm of bees overtakes a hive, but instead of sweetness she experienced sorrow. She, like her family, hoped Christmas in the mountains would be a new beginning for her.

The sound of a truck backing into their driveway caught Julya's attention, and she parted the gingham curtains over the wash basin to see a young man Scott had hired to deliver a cord of wood. The setting sun cast crimson shadows across the fellow's path as he approached the porch.

While the men stacked the extra wood, Julya added the final touches to her torte. She decided to wait on decorating the tree until the family arrived to maintain their tradition of designing it together. Her sons and daughters-in-law were flying into a nearby mountaintop airstrip, and Scott was going to pick them up while she tended to the food. It would take him at least three hours to make the round trip on the narrow, snow-laden roads.

"Honey, the wood is stacked, and I think I'm going to leave early for the airport," Scott said. "The skies are clearing, but because of all the snowfall the last few days, I want to make sure I can get through Jurgen's Pass."

"Be careful, Scott, and take your time," Julya replied.

She watched her husband as he tapped the snow off his mukluks, dusted off his mackinaw, and walked across the room toward her. His red plaid coat accented both his silver hair and his azure eyes. "Come here, my little snow bunny," Scott cooed playfully. Then taking her hands in his, he kissed them both tenderly. "Julya, you are the love of my life. Thank you for being my wife."

"You romantic, you," she responded tersely. Then, in motherly fashion, she scolded, "Scott, you are dripping all over my floor."

"Okay, okay, I'm out of here." He headed across the room, grinning boyishly as he waved to her over his shoulder.

Julya followed Scott to the door and watched him stride down the snowy path toward his vehicle until he disappeared into the forming night shadows. She wanted to call out "I love you, Scott" but couldn't. She felt a wave of sadness spread through her. She was so distracted by her feelings that she hardly noticed the sweep of bitterly cold air engulfing her as she stood in the open door. Scott honked his horn several times as he drove off. Waving in the direction of the car lights, she stepped back inside.

Julya sat down on the pillowed love seat, stared at the fire, and began to pray aloud, "What's wrong with me, Lord, that I can't even express love to my dear husband? And why am I so unhappy? I can't even cry. I wish I could. Perhaps then I would have some relief from this wretchedness I drag around with me. Help me, Lord, help me."

Julya's prayer was cut short by the sound of Scott's returning. She hurried to the window and looked out, wondering what he had forgotten. But the driveway appeared empty, and no car lights shone on the road leading up to the cabin. She listened. The sound intensified. Now it seemed to be more like an approaching train, but Julya wasn't aware of any train tracks still in use in the mountains. Then the cabin began to vibrate. Julya, unsure of what was happening, grabbed the counter to steady herself. Then she felt a huge, earthshaking thump. The cabin was plunged into darkness except for the glimmer from the oil lamps.

She stood still; she could hear her own heart pounding in her ears. The rumbling outside had stopped, but the silence that followed was almost deafening. Julya picked up one of the oil lamps and moved toward the fireplace where she noted a large clot of snow had doused the flames. Then she rushed to the door and slowly opened it. The porch roof swayed precariously, and everywhere Julya looked was a wall of snow. She closed the door and heard the timbers on the porch creak threateningly. Julya trembled as she went to each window and pulled back the curtains. Each window revealed the same scene: an encasement of snow. Her breath caught in her throat as she realized she must be buried. Buried in an avalanche.

Frantic, she paced back and forth as she called out in desperate whispers, "Oh, Lord, no. Don't let me die all alone. Don't let my family find me crushed to death on Christmas Eve. Haven't I gone through enough? Are You going to turn my dream into a nightmare?"

Julya's thoughts darted in and out of strained prayers. She wondered again how this avalanche could have happened. Suddenly she remembered Scott's honking his horn as he drove away. "Oh no, Scott, what have you done to me? Where are you now? You're never there when I need you. I hate you! I hate you!"

Shocked by her passionate admission, Julya stood in the center of the living room with her hand over her mouth, afraid to move. *Maybe I would be better off dead.*

She sunk to the floor, embraced her knees, and began to rock. In the room's shadows, Julya tried to rock away her feelings of despair. Moments passed like hours and then a sound caught Julya's attention. She stopped rocking and listened. The sound was coming from the porch. She stood up, cautiously held the door ajar, and peeked out. The mewing sounds, though still muffled, seemed to emanate from the snow wall directly in front of her. Uncertain how safe the porch was, she opened the door fully and stood in the doorframe to listen.

"It's a cat," Julya announced to herself. She grabbed her sweater off the back of a chair and a plastic bowl from the kitchen table and gingerly stepped onto the weakened porch. Then she squatted and listened. Detecting the area of the stifled cries, she carefully scooped snow and dumped it onto the porch. The groans of the timbers increased her pace.

Julya finally uncovered a paw, then the cat's frightened, frosted face. She tenderly slipped her hand under its back and eased the cat toward her. Once she turned the large calico cat upright, it jumped from her arms and fled into the cabin's safety.

"Ingrate," Julya mumbled, as she crawled back to the door and pulled herself up. Once inside she called, "Here kitty, here kitty. Kitty, kitty, kitty." In the lamplight she spotted the tip of a tail sticking out from under the chair right by her feet. Thinking twice, she closed off the other rooms and then placed a saucer of milk between the fireplace and the chair. Setting the oil lamp on an end table, she sat down and waited, listening to the intimidating silence and wishing she could find a chair big enough to hide under herself.

Julya tried mentally to construct a way out of her confines. She wondered if she could dig her way out, but she wasn't sure where to start. And where would she put all the snow? Would the porch collapse on her? Questions flared up like warning signs as she considered her options.

She wondered how long before Scott would know she was buried in the cabin. Then a thought crossed her mind that terrified her: What if Scott was buried in the avalanche as well?

"No, Lord, please let my husband be safe. He's a good man. I know I said I hated him, but that was just because he didn't rescue me from losing my breast. Even as I say it, I know Scott couldn't do that, but I wanted him to. As unreasonable as that is, that's what I expected."

Julya thought back on the horror and disappointment she had felt when the doctor first had diagnosed her cancer. As she told Scott the news that afternoon, somehow she believed he would help her find a way out of this life-threatening disease without its maiming her. After the surgery Julya found it difficult to respond to Scott's loving touch.

"Meow."

"Well, there you are," Julya said, looking up. "Fine way to show your gratitude, you scamp, hiding under the chair."

The large cat made its way to the saucer and began to lap the milk. After emptying the dish, the calico swaggered over to Julya and sat down on her feet. Julya petted the mottled cat until they were both comfortable with each other. She then wrapped the still shivering animal in an afghan and drew it into her lap. Holding the cat close, she felt they comforted each other with their presence.

"Kitty cat, where did you come from? Who do you belong to? How did you end up outside my porch?" The cat only purred in response and nudged closer. "For now I shall call you my chubby Snowman."

Without the fireplace going, Julya felt chilled. She knelt down on the hearth and looked up the chimney, but even with the oil lamp she couldn't see beyond a few feet. Then she remembered a flashlight in the pantry, and she prayed the batteries would still work. Relief flooded her when the light beamed across the room. Shining it up the smokestack, she saw that the chimney appeared to be open above. Her heart leapt with flickering hope. She quickly set some kindling and then added a couple of logs. The smoke swept up and out the chimney, and soon Julya and her new housemate were toasty warm.

Julya checked the telephone repeatedly, as if hoping it would repair itself. Scott had taken the cell phone, which meant if he was in trouble and still alive, he could call for help. That thought comforted her heart. Then again, Scott might have been far enough away in the minutes before the avalanche covered the cabin that he never realized what had happened. If so, that meant it would be hours before anyone would even try to rescue her. The helpless sense of being trapped pressed in on her ragged emotions.

"Why me, Lord? Wasn't breast cancer enough?" Suddenly the doubts and fears began to tear again at her faith's fabric. "You didn't rescue me then; does that mean You won't now either? Are my prayers futile? Am I going to die in this tomb?"

Womb, it's a womb, child.

The words came to Julya so clearly that they startled her, and she looked around to see if someone was standing beside her. "Womb?" she risked asking.

Wombs bring forth life.

Julya allowed the words to enfold her with warmth. They became a lit candle to her murky soul, and with the illumination came a sense of safety. She pondered the words and wondered if God might be birthing something within her.

"Lord, I realize every time I've been in difficult places I've promised You my undaunted allegiance if You would once again rescue me. Then, when the air cleared and I caught my breath, I would fall back into my self-indulgent ways. But I'm in a very different place since my surgery. I'm so stuck in the mire of despondency."

Anger.

"Anger? I'm sad, Lord, but I don't think I'm angry." Julya's mind replayed her own inflammatory words regarding Scott—"I hate you! I hate you!" Once again she felt the intensity of her statements. Then, slipping off the love seat and onto her knees, she prayed, "Forgive me, Lord, for the anger I've harbored against my husband. How foolish of me to blame him for something he was powerless to change. Only You, Lord, have that kind of…" Julya couldn't finish her thought. In that moment of illuminating truth, she recognized she was also angry with God.

"You know, Lord, You could have rescued me! In a moment, You could have healed me. Where were You when I needed You?" Julya railed at the ceiling. Hearing her own feelings articulated both frightened and relieved her. She waited for the cabin to tumble down on her for such an outburst.

Instead, she heard within her a voice clearer than a mountain stream and purer than a baby's laughter. *I was in the wise counsel of your doctors, the steady hands of your surgeon, the compassionate care of your nurses, the tears of your support group, and the love of your family. I sat through your office visits, I knelt at your bedside, I rejoiced in your recovery. I wept at your anger, and I felt your anguish.*

Tears trickled down Julya's face. Soon the trickle turned into a fountain that allowed her to pour out her grief, disappointment, and anger. She lamented until finally, in exhaustion, her wails turned to gentle sobs, and then she became still. The quiet that followed rested on her like a holy mantle. How long she lay there in His presence she didn't know—perhaps an hour or maybe two. Somehow, where she was or how long she had been there didn't matter. Only who she was with.

She arose to Snowman's cries, muffled cries coming from behind the boxes of decorations in the corner. "What do you think you're doing back there?" Julya lectured gently as she reached over the boxes. Tucked under the branches of the Christmas tree, Snowman's huge eyes looked up at Julya. Then she looked more closely.

"Well, excuse me, but you aren't a Snowman after all, are you? I should say not, Mrs. Snow-mama. Look at all your babies! One, two, three…wait, oh my, four little ones. I'd better find them a warm bed and pour you another saucer of milk."

After lining a wood box with papers and towels, Julya placed Snow-mama and her babies inside and stood over them. Watching the new life stirred something deep inside of Julya...joy.

Suddenly she felt like singing. At the top of her lungs she began to belt out, "Joy to the world, the Lord has come..." She stopped mid-sentence when she heard someone calling her name.

"Julya! Julya, can you hear me?"

Julya ran to the door and called into the wall of snow, "Yes, I can hear you, Scott!"

"We're going to get you out of there! Don't worry," he shouted, sound-ing worried himself. "Are you okay?"

"Yes, we're fine."

"Did you say 'we,' Julya?"

"Yes, I've had a couple of Christmas visitors," she answered jubilantly.

"The boys are with me. We should be able to move through this snow in about an hour."

"The porch is unstable; you better dig for the kitchen window. And Scott..."

"Yes?"

"I love you."

Dear Reader,

If you've chanced on any of my previous writings, you know that *Stardust on My Pillow* looks different from my other books, and for good reason. This is my maiden journey into fiction, and I've loved the trip. Writing fiction for me is like standing on my tiptoes to catch falling stars and skipping across clouds to slide down rainbows.

Some of the stories in *Stardust* have flowed from my fingertips with ease, while others I've squeezed out one word at a time. But all of them have one thing in common: They have surprised me. The characters took over and demanded to be heard.

Banty McCluster in "Runaway" skipped town and ended up smack-dab in the midst of an explosive dilemma. I warned her to beware of her traveling companions, but would she listen to me? Oh no. And the next thing you know... Well, if you've read the story you already know.

Miss Lorna was another gal who felt she had to make a statement of her own. I can understand, considering the whole town of Blessing had developed such a mind-set against her, but a person can state her case in ways besides perching atop the water tower or pilfering the neighbors' Salvation Army donations. Yet, when I tried to explain the finer points of socialization, Lorna flipped her lime green scarf over her right shoulder and sauntered away.

Yes, fiction is, for me, a topsy-turvy adventure in which imagination and principles meet and marry under the fragrant magnolia tree. Fiction is adult fun for the kid in us all. It allows us to twirl around in someone else's tutu as that person's life spins in and out of control. And we get to learn from her tenuous pirouettes without endangering ourselves.

As I wrote each story, I pictured you donning casual dress in preparation for a comfy reading experience. To be specific, I envisioned pajamas. And you surrounded with a plethora of pillows and a cozy comforter. And, oh yes, to make the experience really special, I wanted to whisper to you, "Don't forget the stardust." I hope you didn't!

Sweet dreams,

Patsy